"How Do You Know I'm Not Married?"

Morgan asked.

"I can always tell," he answered with a maddening smile.

"Maybe *you're* married," she said, and he laughed.

"Ask anybody in town, if you're worried," he said, grinning.

"I wasn't *worried*," she replied, emphasizing the last word.

"Curious?" he said, the grin still in place.

Morgan didn't answer.

"I have to get my work done," she finally replied.

"Of course." He nodded, unoffended. She could see that she wasn't fooling him for a minute. The current of mutual attraction flowed between them like the charged air before a thunderstorm, and he knew she was feeling it as much as he was.

Dear Reader:

Welcome! You hold in your hand a Silhouette Desire—your ticket to a whole new world of reading pleasure.

A Silhouette Desire is a sensuous, contemporary romance about passions, problems and the ultimate power of love. It is about today's woman—intelligent, successful, giving—but it is also the story of a romance between two people who are strong enough to follow their own individual paths, yet strong enough to compromise, as well.

These books are written by, for and about every woman that you are—wife, mother, sister, lover, daughter, career woman. A Silhouette Desire heroine must face the same challenges, achieve the same successes, in her story as you do in your own life.

The Silhouette reader is not afraid to enjoy herself. She knows when to take things seriously and when to indulge in a fantasy world. With six books a month, Silhouette Desire strives to meet her many moods, but each book is always a compelling love story.

Make a commitment to romance—go wild with Silhouette Desire!

Best,

Isabel Swift
Senior Editor & Editorial Coordinator

DOREEN OWENS MALEK
Roughneck

Silhouette Desire

Published by Silhouette Books New York

America's Publisher of Contemporary Romance

SILHOUETTE BOOKS
300 East 42nd St., New York, N.Y. 10017

ISBN: 0-373-05450-5

First Silhouette Books printing September 1988

Printed in the U.S.A.

Books by Doreen Owens Malek

DOREEN OWENS MALEK

is a former attorney who decided on her current career when she sold her fledgling novel to the first editor who read it. Since then she has gained recognition for her writing, winning honors from *Romantic Times* magazine and the coveted Golden Medallion Award. She has traveled extensively throughout Europe, Mexico and South America, but it was in her home state of New Jersey that she met and married her college sweetheart. They now make their home in Pennsylvania.

One

Morgan Taylor tapped her fingers on the hotel night-stand as she listened to the ringing of the other end of the phone. She cradled the receiver against her shoulder and stared out the window at the Louisiana sunshine, wondering what excuse Landry's secretary would invent for her this time.

"Landry Associates," the woman answered on an upbeat note, her tone warm but professional.

"Hello, this is Attorney Taylor again," Morgan said. "I wonder if Mr. Landry is available to speak to me now?"

"I'm sorry, ma'am," the woman said promptly. "Mr. Landry is out of the office this afternoon."

Morgan sighed and looked at the ceiling. She and the disembodied telephone voice had been playing this game for two days. Landry was constantly unavailable to take her calls. He was in a meeting, on another line, gone to lunch, out of the office. Either the man was busier than God on the first day of creation or he was dodging her.

"Have you left my messages?" Morgan asked patiently.

"Oh, yes. I reported all of your calls."

Morgan decided that it was time for a more direct approach. "All right, thank you," she said. "Goodbye." She hung up the phone, put aside her briefcase, and went to the closet to get her suit jacket. She would sit in Landry's office and wait for him. Even if he really were gone, he would have to show up sooner or later. If she had to trip him on his way past her, she would make sure her journey from the great Northeast to Bienville, Louisiana, was not in vain.

Morgan was an attorney for TransAmerican Insurance, a Philadelphia-based insurance conglomerate that specialized in underwriting high-risk businesses for substantial premiums. She'd joined the legal staff of the company right out of law school and had been practicing for three years.

She glanced in the mirror above the dresser, smoothed her hair, and straightened the rapidly wilting collar of her blouse. The temperature outside the air-conditioned hotel room was a blazing, humid ninety-five, and Morgan dreaded going out into the streets. But go she must, and she was determined to arrive at Landry's office looking as fresh as possible. She reapplied lipstick to her mouth, pressing her lips together, thinking that she was going to run this phantom to earth, and that it would happen today.

Morgan was in Bienville on the Sunlite Petroleum case, the first major assignment she'd been given to handle alone. Sunlite, insured by TransAmerican, was being sued in a class action. The plaintiffs were the surviving family members of Mexican laborers who had died in an explosion on the Sunlite drilling works. The suit alleged that the accident was caused by negligence on the part of Sunlite, and it was Morgan's job to determine whether TA should settle out of court. The alternative was to go to trial on the merits of Sunlite's case, a trial that Sunlite, and TA, could lose in a big way if the decision went against them.

Morgan picked up her purse and slung the strap over her shoulder, wondering why her key witness was being so elusive. Landry was an independent contractor with his own geophysical surveying company. He'd been brought in by Sunlite to sink a well on the Bienville site, and he had observed the accident firsthand. Morgan knew that his testimony was crucial because he was not an employee of Sunlite; as a free agent with nothing to gain from company loyalty he would have more influence over a judge and jury. She had to interview him and find out what he had to say about the case before she could decide how to handle it.

She descended to the lobby in the hotel elevator and asked for directions to Landry's office at the desk. When she pushed through the revolving door into the street she met a wall of heat. Bienville was sleeping on this sweltering July afternoon and she was one of only a few pedestrians. She walked down the main street and turned left at the pharmacy onto Juniper Street, where she could see the brick facade of Landry's office building shimmering in the distance. She sighed and plodded toward it, feeling the radiation from the pavement frying the soles of her feet, the relentless beating of the sun on her uncovered head. By the time she reached the ground floor of Landry's brownstone she was damp.

The cool marble of the entry hall felt good against her skin as she pressed her forehead to the wall, thinking that if Landry wasn't to be found upstairs she was going to ferret him out with a buffalo gun. She located his name on the glass-covered roster and proceeded to the second floor, where she bypassed the startled receptionist and confronted the secretary who sat outside an office with a frosted door.

"I'm Attorney Morgan Taylor," she announced without preliminaries. "We spoke on the phone this morning."

The woman stiffened and opened her mouth.

"I know," Morgan said wearily, "he isn't in, right?"

The secretary shut her mouth again.

"Then I'll wait for him." Morgan looked around for a place to sit.

"He won't be back for the rest of the day," the woman said hastily.

"Look," Morgan said. She set her briefcase on the floor and pulled her handkerchief out of her pocket. "I'll save us both some time. You tell me where he is and I'll go track him down, okay?" She dabbed at her forehead and blotted her upper lip.

"I couldn't possibly do that."

"Why not?"

"Mr. Landry had several stops to make and...."

"Are you telling me that he didn't leave word where he could be reached, Miss, uh, Hastings?" Morgan asked, reading the woman's nameplate on the desk.

Miss Hastings didn't reply, stymied.

Morgan tried to manufacture a stern manner. "Miss Hastings, I'm sure you know that I want to see Mr. Landry in connection with a legal matter, and I will get a subpoena duces tecum if I have to."

Miss Hastings looked properly abashed.

"It might even be necessary to get a preliminary injunction," Morgan added for further effect, hoping that Miss Hastings wasn't an evening law student about to see through her smoke screen.

"You do realize Mr. Landry could be charged with obstruction of justice."

Miss Hastings bit her lip.

"And contempt of court," Morgan threw in rashly.

Miss Hastings crumbled.

"He's at the Roughneck down on the corner," the secretary burst out.

"The Roughneck?" Morgan said doubtfully.

"It's a...meeting place, sort of a...restaurant and..."

"Bar?" Morgan suggested helpfully.

Miss Hastings nodded.

"Do you mean to tell me," Morgan said in a strong voice, "that while I have been standing here fencing with you this guy has been hiding from me in a saloon?"

"Well," Miss Hastings said feebly, "not hiding exactly, he often goes down there at the end of the day to..."

"Get loaded?"

"Unwind." Miss Hastings looked as though she wished she were unwinding in a similar fashion.

"Fine," Morgan said, holding up her hand in a gesture of surrender. "I get the picture. You say this place is down at the corner?"

"Yes."

"I'll find it." Assuming, Morgan thought to herself as she picked up her briefcase again, that I don't die of sunstroke on the way.

She spent a mercifully short, but hellish, five minutes out in the glare of the sun before she located the Roughneck, a wooden structure with an Acadian roof and an assortment of beer signs blinking in the darkened windows. She pushed through the swinging doors and entered a blessed oasis of coolness filled with the husky babble of masculine voices. She paused, waiting for her eyes to adjust to the gloom. A hush fell around her, and once she could see again she was able to determine why.

Bienville, she knew, meant "good town," and it was clear that this good town was filled with good old boys, a fair number of whom were at this moment in the Roughneck, staring at her.

She was the only woman in the place.

Morgan gripped her briefcase more tightly and marched over to the bar, where a burly man in a white apron was wiping glasses with a flourish.

He grinned at her.

"Help you, ma'am?" he drawled.

Morgan felt the eyes boring into her back, and in the floor-to-ceiling mirror behind the bar she could see the rapt faces watching their exchange.

"I'm looking for Mr. Beauregarde Landry," she said stiffly.

"Is that a fact?" the bartender said with mild interest. He continued to polish a brandy snifter with lazy concentration, putting on a show for his audience.

"Yes. Can you direct me to him?"

The bartender squinted over her head at the paneled rear wall and pretended to think. "Don't know that I can," he replied, as if puzzled.

"Look," Morgan said wearily, tiring of the game, "I know he's here, his secretary told me where to find him. Now are you going to point him out or do I have to ask somebody else?"

"Best ask somebody else," the man said equably, enjoying her discomfiture, totally unruffled. His smile widened.

Morgan wanted to hit him. She turned on her heel and marched to the nearest table. Her progress provoked a storm of whistles and catcalls and she could feel her face flushing.

"Is Mr. Landry here?" she asked of the first man she saw.

He looked over his shoulder, and as he did a man rose from the table behind them.

"I'm Landry," the latter said, mercifully ending the search. "May I help you?"

Morgan skirted the forest of table and chair legs that separated them and presented herself to the speaker. He was surrounded by a litter of beer bottles and a group of men, who fell silent, fascinated.

"I'm Attorney Morgan Taylor," she announced briskly. "I represent TransAmerican Insurance and I've been trying to get in touch with you for the past two days. I wonder if I might have a word?"

Landry looked her over, taking in the tailored blue suit and sensible pumps, the voluminous shoulder bag, the leather briefcase. He wasn't laughing, as some of his companions were, but his lips twitched dangerously.

Morgan gazed back at him steadily. He was tall and lean, dark, with a deep suntan that made him appear even darker. His anthracite hair was casually, if artfully, layered, and his long-lashed light brown eyes were the color of watered whiskey. He was wearing jeans, boots, and a plaid shirt.

"I thought Morgan Taylor was a man," he said to her.

Morgan took the hand he offered her and shook it.

"Your eyesight must be failin', Beau," one of his companions chortled. The rest of the men at the table nudged each other and chuckled.

"I never met the lady," Landry said, smiling slightly.

"Because you've dodged me for forty-eight hours," Morgan informed him crisply.

"I wouldn't have," he said evenly, "if I'd seen you."

This prompted more commentary and suggestive laughter from the group.

"Knock it off," Landry said to them easily, and to Morgan's astonishment, they did.

"Is there some place we can talk?" she said pointedly.

Landry turned. "Come into the next room," he said. "It's quiet in there."

Morgan followed him through a door into a deserted banquet hall adjacent to the bar. The conversation from next door was still audible, but considerably muted. He left the door ajar and pulled out a chair from under an empty table, holding it for her. She slid into it and he dropped into one across from her.

"What did Larry say to you?" he asked her curiously, stretching his long legs and folding his arms.

"Larry?"

"The bartender."

"I asked him where you were and he wouldn't tell me," Morgan said.

"Why not?" Landry asked.

Morgan sighed. "I think he was enjoying the floor show. As long as I was wandering around helplessly trying to find you, he and his pals were getting a good laugh."

Landry thought that over but didn't comment. He waited in silence until Morgan asked him, "Why have you been avoiding me, Mr. Landry?"

He shrugged. "Don't like lawyers. Don't like insurance companies." He leaned back and laced his fingers behind his head. "I especially don't like lawyers who *work* for insurance companies."

Morgan had heard this before and ignored it. "Mr. Landry," she began again.

"Call me Beau," he said.

"Mr. Landry," she repeated firmly, and he grinned.

"Ma'am?" he said, raising his black brows.

"Don't you want to help with the Sunlite case?" she inquired.

"No," he replied shortly, his smile fading.

"Why not?"

"I'm not going to *help* you fleece the families of those dead guys out of their claim," Landry said flatly, his gaze locked with hers.

"You misunderstand my intention," Morgan said.

"I don't think so." His smoky amber eyes were hard.

Morgan folded her hands on the table before her and leaned forward. "Mr. Landry, your preconceived ideas about my profession are clouding your judgment. It's possible for this matter to be settled out of court. The plaintiffs could be awarded a substantial sum without ever having the hassle and expense, much less the emotional strain, of going to court."

"That sounds like a real pat speech, lady," Landry observed. "How often do you use it?"

Morgan felt her temper flare, but tried not to show it. "It happens to be the truth," she replied calmly.

"Who's going to award them this *substantial sum*, huh? Your bosses, out of the goodness of their corporate hearts?" Landry asked sarcastically.

"The amount would be fixed by mutual agreement, with court approval," Morgan answered stiffly.

"And this *amount* would be far less than they'd get if they went to trial, right?" Landry asked shrewdly, his eyes narrowed.

"Not necessarily," Morgan said, disregarding the way he italicized her expressions when he used them himself.

"What do you mean by that?"

Morgan lifted one shoulder expressively. "Juries are capricious."

"So?"

"I've seen people get much less than they deserved because they insisted on going to court and then fared badly there. Anything can happen. Supposedly reliable witnesses perform erratically, the judge gives poor instructions, sound objections are overruled, the plaintiff comes off as unsympathetic..." She gestured vaguely and let the sentence trail off into silence.

"I get it now," Landry said coldly. "You and the head honchos up there in Philly are really trying to do these poor ignorant people a favor. Now why do you suppose I can't see it that way?"

"Perhaps because you're hopelessly biased?" Morgan suggested frostily.

Unexpectedly, Landry smiled. "Relax, lady. If your face freezes that way you're going to be in big trouble."

"Mr. Landry, I really wish you would confine your remarks to the matter at hand."

"You talk just like a lawyer," Landry said, smiling slightly.

"I am a lawyer."

"Never did meet one who had a sense of humor."

"When you say something funny, maybe I'll laugh."

They stared at each other across the expanse of oak table, equally unyielding. Morgan noticed a tiny horse-shoe-shaped scar on his chin, darkly shadowed by his beard. His black hair was so thick and shiny that it reflected the minimal overhead lighting with a dull patina. Morgan deliberately looked away.

"Can we set aside your opinions for a moment and deal with the facts?" she finally said, trying again.

Landry didn't answer. The crash of drums next door signaled the start of a musical interlude. A Tex-Mex band began to play a Los Lobos tune at an ear-splitting decibel level. A group near to the shared wall sang along, badly. The din contrasted sharply with the stony silence enveloping the two sitting alone in the vacant banquet hall.

Landry got up and closed the door between the rooms firmly, cutting off the concert. He pushed his hair off his forehead wearily as he sat down again and said with resignation, "What exactly do you want me to do?"

Caught off guard by his sudden capitulation, Morgan paused a moment and then said eagerly, "Let me interview you, take a deposition."

"What's that?" Landry said suspiciously.

"You answer a list of prepared questions, under oath, just like in court."

"Your questions?"

"Yes."

He shook his head. "I don't know," he said doubtfully.

Morgan mentally counted to ten. She folded her hands carefully and leaned forward. "Mr. Landry, it's clear that you believe Sunlite, my insured, is in the wrong here."

"Your insured?" he repeated, raising one dark brow.

"You do think the oil company was negligent," Morgan said patiently, refusing to be baited.

"Negligent as hell," Landry replied grimly. "I'll never work for that outfit again."

"You observed this negligence yourself?"

"That's right."

"Fine. I'm going to give you an opportunity to say so. In writing. I'll take your deposition, and my other findings, back to Philadelphia, and it's entirely possible the plaintiffs will get exactly what they want, without a trial."

"You giving me the straight story?" Landry suddenly said in an intimate tone. He leaned forward, his gaze locking with hers.

Morgan stared back at him, nonplussed. This sudden switch from semibelligerence to forthright inquiry was unsettling.

"Yes," she said softly, seduced in spite of herself.

"Then I guess you're not representing your, uh, insured very well," he observed flatly.

"I'm just trying to get at the truth," Morgan replied. "And if the truth looks bad for Sunlite, we'll pay up front rather than go to court. A fair amount, too; we don't want it contested later."

"I see," he said slowly, nodding. Then, "Tell me what's involved."

"We make an appointment to get together...."

"Dinner tomorrow night," he said promptly.

Morgan stopped, flustered. "I think it's better if we keep this entirely on a professional basis."

Landry put his palms flat on the table between them. "Those are my terms. Take them or leave them. If you want your disposition—"

"Deposition," Morgan corrected.

"Whatever. There's the deal."

"That's extortion."

He pushed his chair back and crossed his legs at the ankles, smiling with satisfaction. "Sounds like a big fancy word for a little business meeting."

"Is that what it's going to be?" Morgan asked warily.

"What are you worried about, *chère*?" he drawled. "Think I'll kidnap you and that briefcase and neither one of you will ever see Philadelphia again?"

Morgan could feel her face growing warm. He was making her feel foolish and she didn't like it. He knew exactly what she meant and his pretended ignorance was infuriating; the line between business and pleasure was clear in her mind and she became uncomfortable when it blurred.

"I'll go with you as long as we both understand that it's not a date," she said primly, and then wished instantly she could call the words back. She sounded unbearably priggish to her own ears, and her blush worsened considerably.

To her utter chagrin, he burst out laughing.

"I promise I'll explain to the hostess and the waiter and the wine steward, and everyone else in the restaurant, that it's not a date," he said solemnly as soon as he'd recovered. Then he started to chuckle again. "I'll tell the doorman and the parking attendant, too, if you like," he added, with an impish grin. "We wouldn't want anyone to be confused."

"Is this how you usually conduct your social life?" Morgan asked testily, feeling ridiculous, as he intended, and stalling for time.

"I thought this wasn't going to be a social outing," he said teasingly, then sobered when he saw her expression. "Let's say I suit my tactics to the occasion," he added in a more responsive tone.

"And this one calls for blackmail?" she asked.

Again he startled her by switching lanes abruptly. "I want you to go out with me," he said directly, with no trace of humor. "I thought if I asked you for a date, you would say no, but if I combined it with your work, which you obviously take so seriously, you would be forced to say yes. Was I wrong?"

Morgan met his eyes. "You were not wrong," she said quietly.

"Then we're on?" he asked.

"How do you know I'm not married?" she asked.

"You're not married," he said confidently.

"How can you be so sure?" she asked, annoyed.

"I can always tell," he answered obliquely, with a maddening smile, and Morgan's pique returned.

"Maybe you're married," she said, and he laughed again.

"Ask anybody in town if you're worried," he said, grinning.

"I wasn't worried," she replied, emphasizing the last word.

"Curious?" he said, the grin still in place.

Morgan didn't answer.

"From a professional viewpoint, of course," he amended, his eyes widening innocently.

"What time?" Morgan asked grimly.

"Does that mean the answer's yes?" he asked, watching her face.

Morgan hesitated. Despite his noticeable lack of enthusiasm for both her profession and her employer, he intrigued her.

"I have to get my work done," she replied.

"Oh, of course," he said, nodding, unoffended. She could see that she wasn't fooling him for a minute. The current of mutual attraction flowed between them like the charged air before a thunderstorm, and he knew she was feeling it as much as he was.

"I'll pick you up at your hotel," he went on. "Where are you staying?"

"At the Regency Château here in Bienville."

Landry stood, satisfied. "Antoine's okay?"

"Fine." The name meant nothing to her.

"Don't forget your deposition." He pulled her chair out for her and she rose, shouldering her purse.

"I won't," she said.

"Oh, and one more thing. Do you ever take off that uniform?"

Morgan stared at him. "I beg your pardon?"

He grinned. "I only mean that if you're wearing that suit when I pick you up tomorrow night I'm going to make you join the army."

She had to laugh. He was just too outrageous.

He led her through the saloon and as they passed the barman Landry said to him, "Hey Larry, the next time a lady asks for me, you tell her where I am, you hear?"

Larry looked first startled, then alarmed. "Sure, Beau," he said nervously, his eyes sliding to Morgan and then back to Landry.

"Good," Landry agreed easily, but Morgan didn't mistake the undertone of menace in Landry's voice. She sensed a core of steel beneath his casual manner, and the bartender's reaction confirmed it. This man was not the type of boardroom influence peddler she was used to dealing with in Philadelphia. His power was more earthly and elemental, fed by an internal fire. She shivered slightly as he touched her back while handing her through the door. What on earth was she doing going to dinner with him, a business contact, a man she'd just met?

The fierce sunlight blinded her for a moment as they stepped outside, and he loomed in front of her, a cutout figure in a shadow play. Then she shielded her eyes with her hand and his features emerged, the glossy black hair shining with highlights, the dark eyes framed with long, silky lashes, tangled in places like a child's.

"I'll walk you back to the hotel," he said softly.

Morgan shook her head. "No, I have a couple of stops to make first," she said hastily. It was the truth, but she also felt an immediate need to get away from him, as if in another minute she might do or say something she would later regret.

"All right," he said. "Eight o'clock, then."

"Eight o'clock," she repeated.

He lifted his hand in farewell, smiled slightly, and went back inside the bar.

Morgan looked after him for a moment, then hurried off down the street. She had brought only business clothes, nothing suitable for a social occasion, and as she passed the glass storefronts she looked for a shop where she might purchase a dinner dress. She passed everything else, including a butcher's shop and a dentist's office, before she finally found something called "Bobbie Jo's Boutique," and, about to drop from heat exhaustion, she staggered inside.

A saleswoman descended on her immediately. Bobbie Jo and company did not let any grass grow when a prospective customer appeared.

"Hello," the clerk beamed. "May I help you?"

"Hi," Morgan gasped, wiping her perspiring brow with her rumpled handkerchief. Her briefcase slipped from her hand and hit the carpeted floor with a muffled thud. She leaned against the peach-flowered wallpaper and let the chilly breath of the air conditioning flow over her skin like balm.

"Y'all feeling poorly?" the clerk asked, concerned.

"Hot out there," Morgan replied weakly, attempting a smile.

"Regular summer day," the woman replied mildly. Her accent transformed the phrase into "Reg'lah summah die."

"Humid," Morgan said, beginning to recover slightly. The word was inadequate. She'd felt as though she were struggling through a vat of petroleum jelly.

"Oh, sure," the woman agreed. "New Orleans is surrounded by water. The gulf and the river, Lake Pontchartrain, the bayous...."

Morgan didn't want to think about the bayous. They loomed in her mind like some vast inland swamp, infested with snakes, alligators and mosquitoes, the Loch Ness monster on a world tour for all she knew. "I need a dress," she said quickly.

"You came to the right place," the lady said, indicating the well-stocked racks along the walls.

"For a dinner at..." Morgan paused, trying to remember the name of the restaurant Landry had mentioned. "Antoine's," she concluded.

"Antoine's," the clerk said, impressed. "Well, that's a right fancy place, down in the Quarter. Do you have anything in mind?"

"Sleeveless," Morgan said decisively. "Lightweight."

"Something in silk?"

"Sounds good."

The saleslady led her to a rack. "Size ten?" she guessed, gesturing.

"Usually," Morgan agreed, surveying the merchandise. She quickly selected a number of items and handed them to the clerk, who led the way to a changing booth.

"You're from up north, aren't you?" she asked as Morgan pulled the curtain closed and began to disrobe.

"Is it that obvious?" Morgan replied.

"From the way you talk. And your reaction to the weather."

"I see. You know, it gets humid in Philadelphia, too, but not like this." Morgan hung her damp garments on the hook provided and wished she had been able to shower before this shopping trip. She began to try on the dresses she'd chosen, and when she found one she liked she emerged from the booth to model it for the clerk.

"Oh, that's wonderful," the woman beamed. "That just came in new last week. Such a lovely color for you."

Morgan turned in front of the three-way mirror on the selling floor and had to agree. The muted rose shade flattered her shoulder-length dark blond hair and blue eyes and brought out the peach tones in her fair skin. The sleeveless silk sheath had a V neck with a slight décolletage and a slit in the back of the hem to expose her slim legs. A light collarless jacket of the same featherweight material fell to fingertip length. It was perfect.

Morgan charged it with reckless abandon, deciding she would worry about the cost when she got home. For reasons she did not wish to examine too closely, she wanted to look smashing for dinner the next evening.

The saleslady, thrilled with such a quick commission, practically bowed Morgan out of the shop. On the way back to the hotel Morgan stopped in a store called "Dixieland Drugs" and bought a lipstick to match the dress and a new tube of mascara. Thus armed, she felt ready to take on her upcoming encounter with Beauregarde Landry.

Once in her room, she tossed her purchases on the bed and took a long, cool shower, washing her hair and dressing in an ancient kimono from college days. She called her office for her messages and then ordered dinner in her room.

She intended to spend the evening doing paperwork and didn't plan to think about Beau Landry again.

Landry unlocked the door of his office, rattling his keys, and switched on the overhead light. Miss Hastings and the receptionist had gone home, and he headed for the pile of messages on his desk, smiling as he sifted through the stack of pink slips. There were several from Morgan Taylor. She had evidently tried to get through for a while by phone, and then put on her serious business outfit and tracked him down in person.

His smile widened as he remembered the determined expression she wore while she threaded through the exclusively male preserve of the Roughneck, carrying her briefcase like a weapon. Another woman might have been put off by the idea of entering a bar full of oil field workers, especially in search of a man who had been trying to avoid her, but Ms. Taylor appeared to be an unusual woman. Although obviously uncomfortable in the bar, her goal had been more important than her embarrassment, and she'd accomplished what she'd set out to do.

He found that interesting.

She was pretty, too, not in a flashy way, but in a subtle, ladylike way that reminded him of the china figurines his mother had collected when he was a child. This impression was enhanced by her clipped, Northern accent and professional manner. He'd never met a lady lawyer; he'd had as little as possible to do with the breed in general, regarding them as thieves in suits, to be avoided at all costs. Now he was making an exception in the case of this cool, direct blonde, partly because he really was curious about what she had to say regarding the Sunlite case, but mostly because she fascinated him. He was bored with seductive, coquettish females who batted their eyelashes and strutted their stuff like cocker spaniels in a kennel show. She was the opposite, dressed down, barely made-up, and demure.

He'd newly discovered that he was a sucker for demure.

He sat down in his swivel chair and picked up the phone to return some of his calls.

He was looking forward to seeing Morgan Taylor again.

Two

Morgan brushed her hair furiously and stared into the mirror, willing the flyaway blond mass to behave. Her usually cooperative tresses had chosen this occasion to grow out from the side of her head over one temple, giving her a lopsided appearance. A topknot always made her feel like Pebbles Flintstone, so she finally settled on a chignon, and added pearl studs to her exposed ears with cold fingers. She was very nervous.

Beau Landry was due to pick her up in a few minutes, and she was rethinking the whole arrangement. She must have been in an altered state to agree to this; she should have insisted on deposing him in the sterile atmosphere of his office. The thought of spending an entire evening with him, making social chitchat in a restaurant, added to her sense of impropriety. It was all wrong.

She turned abruptly at the sound of a knock on her door. She might as well face up to what she had done; she could hardly hide in the bathroom until the man went away. She crossed the room and opened the door, her pulse leaping.

Morgan's heartbeat returned to normal with a sense of anticlimax when she saw that it was only the bellboy.

"Miss Taylor?" he said.

"Yes."

He handed her a slim white box. Puzzled, Morgan tipped him automatically and took off the cover as the door closed behind him.

Inside was single yellow rose wrapped in tissue, with a note.

"I'm waiting for you down in the lobby," it said. It was signed "B. Landry."

Seduced in spite of herself, Morgan was smiling slightly as she sniffed the delicate blossom and put it into a bathroom glass filled with water. Was this the fabled Southern charm she'd been hearing about? If so, it was pretty potent stuff.

She picked up her purse and glanced at her afterthought hairdo in the mirror. It actually looked quite nice. Thus fortified, she headed out to the elevator.

Landry was lounging against the downstairs wall, his hands in his pockets, his eyes on the sliding doors. He straightened when he saw her and came forward, taking her hand.

"You look lovely," he said.

"Thank you."

"Did you get my note?"

"Of course. The flower was a very nice touch."

He glanced at her alertly. "Too much?" he said.

Morgan looked back at him levelly. "I don't understand."

"Yes, you do." His lips held the barest trace of a smile. "You think it was overkill, and you're deliberately unimpressed."

Morgan returned his smile. "Oh, I was impressed. Who wouldn't be?" Her tone was even, slightly cool.

He chuckled, then sighed. "Okay, *chère*. I promise to knock off the Lothario act if you promise to defrost that smile a few degrees. Deal?"

Morgan laughed. "It's a deal." He was difficult to resist. Dressed in a beige linen suit with an eggshell shirt and a striped tie in shades of brown, he looked like an advertisement for tropical lime after-shave.

"And no lawyer talk until after dinner," he added, pressing his advantage.

"Now, wait a minute. I didn't agree to that," Morgan replied. "The lawyer talk is the *purpose* of this dinner."

"Only in your opinion," Landry replied. "In mine, it's a compromise. No legal discussion, no date, remember? The least you can do is let me pretend that you wanted to be with me until the coffee arrives, okay?"

His tone was a little testy, and Morgan realized that he resented the condition she had put on the evening. He probably wasn't used to women giving him a tough time.

"Okay," she said quietly, and his expression relaxed.

They were still in the lobby, and the flow of guests eddied past them, the women's high heels clicking on the marble-tiled floor. Morgan could see the reflection of Landry's back in a gilt-edged mirror behind him. His shoulders were broad, his waist narrow, and his jacket conformed to his body contours as if made for them. Which it undoubtedly had been. Her eyes shifted back to his face, and she saw that he was watching her expectantly.

"Shall we go?" he said, gesturing toward the door.

"Yes, of course." Morgan crossed the plant-filled lobby with him, her shoes silenced as they walked on the figured Oriental rug. The doorman was waiting at the curb with Landry's car, a dark European sedan, its chrome gleaming in the summer dusk. Morgan took the passenger seat. The rich leather upholstery caressed her legs as Landry slid in next to her, seeming suddenly very large in the confined space.

"Comfortable?" he said as he shifted the idling car into gear.

"Yes, perfectly," Morgan replied. "How long is the trip to Antoine's?"

"About twenty-five, thirty minutes," he replied.

"Thirty minutes?" She'd thought it was around the corner.

"To New Orleans."

"Oh." Of course. The restaurant was in New Orleans. That's what the saleslady had meant about "the Quarter." Why didn't she pay attention to these details? Now she was trapped in a car with this man for half an hour, in addition to their time at dinner. Her mouth was beginning to go dry and her tongue was sticking to the roof of her mouth, not exactly an aid to conversation. What was she going to say to him?

"Do you like being a lawyer?" Landry asked her suddenly as they glided to a stop at a light.

Morgan considered how to reply. "I've never done anything else," she finally said. "I have no basis of comparison."

"Doesn't it bother you, the way people feel about lawyers, I mean?" he asked.

"How do people feel about lawyers?" Morgan asked stiffly, staring straight ahead.

"You know," he said, gunning the motor as the light changed.

"No, I don't," Morgan said, turning her head to look at him. "Apparently you think everyone feels the way you do, and you're wrong."

He held up a placating hand. "All right, *chère*, all right. Forget I said anything. I'm not trying to pick a fight."

"Could have fooled me," Morgan muttered.

"I heard that," he said, grinning.

"Good."

"I think I'm kind of getting off on the wrong foot here," Landry added, his smile lessening slightly.

"What was your first clue?" Morgan asked him.

He pursed his lips. "Want to change the subject?"

"That's probably a good idea."

"Would you like to hear about all my crazy ancestors? That's a guaranteed icebreaker."

Morgan glanced at him again to see if he was serious. He appeared to be. "Your crazy ancestors?" she said tentatively.

"Sure thing." He downshifted for the entrance ramp onto the highway. "What'll it be?"

"Be?"

"Who would you like to hear about? My great-great-granddaddy Amos who held off the Yankees with a sharpened crochet hook? Or his sister Belinda who buried the family silver in the riverbed when the Union soldiers arrived? Then she couldn't find it until a fork floated by the summer house during Reconstruction and she remembered where she'd put it."

"Belinda," Morgan said, sure he was making it all up.

"Well," Landry began, taking a breath, "Auntie Bee, as she is known in the family, was a little addled before the war began and, believe me, by the time it was over she was gone entirely. She lived to be ninety-two and during the last ten years of her life supported herself by giving walk-throughs of the homestead, which by then was falling down, to the tourists. She used to serve them sherry in little crystal glasses and distribute samples of the Confederate money she'd found in the attic.''

Morgan listened, entranced. It had to be true; nobody had that fertile an imagination.

''By the time my relatives found out what she was doing,'' Landry went on, ''and told her that the Confederate currency was valuable, she had given it all away. She was astonished that anybody would pay anything for 'all that old paper.' She was convinced that if it hadn't been worth anything to Jeff Davis it certainly wouldn't be worth anything so many years later.''

''She must have been wonderful,'' Morgan said softly.

''So the story goes. My sister Linda was named for her.''

''It must give you a sense of stability to have such a history.''

''I wouldn't exactly call *my* relatives stable,'' he replied, and they both laughed.

''Well, interesting, anyway,'' Morgan amended.

''They were that, I guess.''

''I'm adopted,'' Morgan said, ''and although my foster parents mean the world to me, I often wonder about my real family, who they were, where they came from, what they were like. You're fortunate to know.''

''Have you ever tried to trace your blood parents?'' Landry asked.

Morgan shook her head. ''I was involved in a few cases like that when I was interning at a firm in Philadelphia, and they're usually painful. The adoptive parents are often hurt by the child's feeling of incompleteness, the need to know about his biological roots. And going back into the past frequently opens old wounds. Children are generally given up for adoption for sound reasons, and rethinking all that twenty or twenty-five years later rarely does anyone any good.''

"It's very kind of you to consider your parents that way,'' he murmured.

"I love them, and I've never felt that I lacked anything,'' Morgan replied. "There's just a certain curiosity that always remains.'' She changed the subject. "Is the house still there?'' she asked. "The house where Belinda found the money?''

"The land is. Only the foundation is left of the original structure. I mean to rebuild it, just the way it was. I've hired an architect to work from the original plans.'' Determination was clear in his voice.

"Where's the property?''

"On the river, near St. Francisville.'' He, like others in the area, referred to the Mississippi as "the river,'' as if there were, and could be, no other. It was the way New Yorkers talked about "the city.''

"Is that where you grew up?'' Morgan asked.

He shook his head. "No, we had lost the family place before my time; it had reverted to the parish for unpaid taxes. I just got the land back last year. I grew up in New Orleans.''

"Oh.'' Morgan's image of him underwent a change. He hadn't always been prosperous, then.

He looked over at her. "Fascinating, right? A real riches-to-rags story.'' His tone was laced with bitterness.

Morgan didn't know what to say.

"My great-great-grandfather was ruined by the Civil War,'' he explained. "His last cotton crop was burned in the boats by the Yankees, and after the surrender, the carpetbaggers picked him clean, finishing the job. The family fortunes never recovered. My ancestors weren't exactly bred to hard work, and when they were left penniless they were as helpless as puppies. My great-grandmother, Amos's daughter, wound up giving piano lessons to the children of the Northern profiteers for grocery money, and her son, my grandfather, was among the last of those colorful riverboat gamblers Hollywood likes to glamorize. He was so colorful, in fact, and such a bad gambler that he eventually lost everything he had. He married late in life and by the time he had my father there was nothing left of the homeplace but the name and a bunch of canceled mortgage papers. My father raised my sister and me in rented rooms in the Quarter.''

Morgan listened in silence, wondering why he was telling her all this. Was he some sort of eccentric who blamed every Yankee for injustices that had occurred over a hundred years ago?

As if reading her mind, his voice softened suddenly as he said, "Don't fret, *chère*. I'm not expecting you to apologize for everybody living north of the Mason-Dixon line, and anyway, some of the changes were for the best. But knowing what went before has made me determined to get some respect back. The Landry clan has harbored its last wastrel.''

Morgan guessed that the final sentence referred to his father but didn't want to ask. She glanced around and realized that they had left the highway.

"Is Antoine's near here?" she asked.

Landry nodded. He was driving through a narrow, congested thoroughfare where the humidity hung in the air like a fine mist, pearlizing the light of the street lamps in the summer dusk. Tiny shops with dusty, clouded windows were wedged in side-by-side with restaurants and antique stores carrying every kind of goods from the past: clothing, furniture, books. Pedestrians jammed the walkways despite the heat, and visitors with cameras strung about their necks like garlands took pictures of everything, the landmarks and the balconies and each other.

"It's very busy, isn't it?" she asked, stating the obvious.

"Tourist trap, this time of year," Landry said, with the cynicism of the jaded native. He angled his car into a minuscule, cobbled side street and then turned again into an alley behind a building. Morgan watched, bewildered, as he put the car in neutral and said, "Just wait here a moment."

He vaulted out of his seat and knocked on a door marked Service that was set neatly into a blank wall. It was opened from inside, and Landry vanished, only to reappear seconds later with his arm around a man in a waiter's fancy uniform. The two approached the car and Landry opened Morgan's door to help her out.

"Pete, this is Morgan Taylor. She's a lawyer from Philadelphia," he said to his companion.

Pete, a graying man in his forties, beamed and said in a pronounced Cajun accent, "How do you do, young lady. Welcome to New Orleans."

Morgan nodded, glancing uncertainly at Landry.

"Pete's a friend of mine," Landry said. "He's going to bring us in through the kitchen so we don't have to deal with that line of tourists waiting to get in out front."

He took Morgan's hand and she followed along dutifully as Pete led them between groaning steam tables and gleaming stainless-steel appliances in the hot, busy room. It was filled with bustling people in white aprons and the

pungent smells of Cajun cooking. They emerged into a
carpeted hallway, where Pete called the maître d' from his
stand and said something in a quick patois that Morgan
couldn't understand. The maître d' nodded and signaled
for Landry to come ahead. As Pete left he said in passing to Landry, "I'll send Billy out for your car."

The maître d' took them past the crowd and into the
main room, which was huge and had a glass wall afford-
ing a view of the river. Morgan hadn't realized they were
so close to the water, but now she could smell it, a rich,
earthy aroma of mud and growing things. It pervaded the
atmosphere, the scented air pouring in from the front
entrance, potent despite the air conditioning. Standing
and hanging plants were everywhere, so patrons appeared to be dining in the midst of a garden. The furniture was white wicker with pale green linens, emphasizing
the elegant, outdoor theme. Morgan half expected to see
ladies in gauzy dresses and picture hats chatting with
gentlemen in white duck pants and boaters; it was like a
scene from Renoir. A single violinist played Vivaldi on a
raised dais at one end of the room, and Morgan spotted
a harp standing behind him. Through the window she
could see an outdoor deck fronting the river, filled with
ice cream tables shielded by striped umbrellas and surrounded by matching canvas chairs. Morgan could imagine that in cooler weather it would be very pleasant to
dine there, observing the tugboats, barges and other craft
heading out into the gulf. The whole effect was magical.

"Do you like it?" Landry asked at her side.

"It's lovely," Morgan replied, meaning it.

The maître d' took them to a secluded table by the
window, set off from the other patrons by a screen of
potted palms. The captain appeared and Landry ordered a bottle of French wine that Morgan was sure she

wouldn't be able to drink. Wine always gave her a head-ache, and the more expensive the vintage, the worse her head a few hours later. This one sounded like it might produce a real skull-banger.

The menu consisted of two cream-bond pages, hand-written with a calligraphy pen, inserted into a tasseled, engraved cover. The dishes were written in French on one page and in English on the other. There were no prices. There was also not a single dish that Morgan had ever tasted in her life. She was beginning to sense that she might be in trouble.

"What do you recommend?" she asked tentatively.

He was watching her, smiling slightly. "Have you ever had Cajun food?" he asked.

"Never."

"Then you're in for a treat."

"Really?" she said faintly.

"Do you doubt it?"

"I've heard it's very spicy."

"We'll keep plenty of ice water on hand," he said dryly.

Morgan shrugged. "I think you'd better choose for me," she finally said, closing the menu and putting it back on the table.

"Fine."

"But tell me what it is before you order," she added hastily.

He grinned. "Don't want any surprises, *chère*?"

Morgan smiled weakly. Strange food contributed to her feeling of alienation from this Southern culture; where was a sirloin steak when she needed one?

The waiter appeared and stood silently behind Landry's shoulder.

"I think we'll start with blackened redfish, then the crawfish gumbo, and a crab *étouffée* for the entrée, with new potatoes and the peas *en roux*," Landry said to Morgan. "Any questions?"

"I don't know if I want to eat anything that's described as 'blackened,'" she said warily.

"That's just the batter coating; it's delicious," Landry assured her.

"And crawfish?" Morgan asked.

"Tastes like shrimp."

"Gumbo?"

"A cross between stew and soup, thickened with okra."

She'd heard of okra. And the crab sounded fine, though she wasn't sure what *étouffée* was. Some sort of stuffing, probably.

"Okay," Morgan agreed. Landry turned to the waiter and rattled off their order in French, but Morgan could tell by his cadence that it wasn't the same language spoken in Paris. The waiter scribbled and departed, to be replaced by the steward with their wine. He uncorked it and poured an ounce of it into Landry's glass for him to taste. Landry nodded and the waiter left the bottle on ice in a silver stand next to their table.

"Would you like some?" Landry asked, wrapping the bottle in its snowy cloth and offering it to her.

"Thank you," Morgan said, not wishing to seem ungracious. She would just sip it to be polite.

Landry filled her glass and replaced the bottle. "So how do you like the South so far?" he asked, raising his own glass to his lips.

"I've been working since I got here, so I haven't seen very much of it," she replied.

"We'll have to remedy that," he said. "How long will you be staying?"

"A few weeks, I think. However long it takes."

"A few weeks, hmm," he said. "Well, the first thing we'll have to arrange is a little riverboat cruise up to Vicksburg," he said. "How does tomorrow night sound?"

"Tomorrow night?" Morgan said, breathless. She'd been telling herself that she would just see him this evening in order to get the deposition, and now here he was arranging another date. He was like a force of nature, carrying her along with him, impossible to block.

"Sure," he said. "The river is beautiful at night, and I have a friend who does an upstream run in a little fake paddle wheeler for the tourists. I'm sure he'll give us a private trip."

"You have a lot of friends," Morgan said, laughing. "And what on earth is a fake paddle wheeler?"

"Oh, it's a boat that's made to look like one of the originals, the Mark Twain type of thing with two open decks and a paddle wheel on the back. It's really powered by a diesel engine."

"I see. The best of both worlds, in a way."

"I guess. It preserves the romantic illusion of the past with all the efficiency of the present."

Morgan surveyed him for a moment, taking in the wide, bourbon-and-branch eyes and the splash of black hair falling onto his forehead. He really was attractive in a dark, challenging way, and admitting that to herself was half the battle in dealing with the emotions he was arousing.

"May I ask you a question?" she said, taking a minuscule sip of her wine.

"Certainly," he replied, holding her gaze.

"You've told me you were born and raised here, but your accent is very slight. You don't sound like the other people I've heard."

"I went to school up north," he answered. "I got a scholarship to a college in Boston, and after that I worked there for several years. I guess I kind of lost the accent along the way."

"Oh, I could still tell you were from the South," Morgan said. "You have that flavor in your speech."

"Flavor?"

"A softness, lilting vowels. It's very...nice," she finished lamely, looking away from him, aware that she had said too much.

"So do you like me, then, or just the way I talk?" he asked quietly, watching her.

"May I take the fifth?" she asked, and he grinned.

"Can you stop being a lawyer for five minutes?" he asked.

"I'll try," she replied meekly.

"Am I gaining ground?" he persisted.

"With what?"

"With you."

Morgan looked up gratefully, spared a reply as the waiter brought the appetizer. Her gratitude vanished when she saw it.

"Looks good," Landry said enthusiastically, picking up his fork.

Morgan stared at him. "It's burnt," she said.

"No it's not," he said, chuckling.

"What are you talking about? It's covered in charcoal."

"Just taste it," he directed.

Morgan obeyed, cutting off a corner of the fish and putting it on the tip of her tongue. Tears sprang to her eyes, but she had no choice but to swallow it. She grabbed for the glass of wine and bolted it, forgetting that it was going to give her a migraine.

"Well?" Landry said devilishly, swallowing a healthy bite.

"Hot," Morgan gasped, blinking.

"Good?"

"No!" she said forcefully, recovering. She shot him a withering look.

Landry shook his head, sighing. "I'm afraid you're just a Yankee sissy," he said, dissecting his fish. "Where do you think this food comes from?"

"Hell?" she suggested, draining her water glass, her mouth still smarting.

"From the best chef in Louisiana. Where's your sense of adventure?" He trapped several of the crumbs from the batter on the tines of his fork and popped them into his mouth.

"I must have left it back on Chestnut Street," Morgan replied. "May I have some more water?" she added pointedly, holding up her empty glass.

"Take mine," he said magnanimously, waving his free hand. "I won't be needing it."

Morgan did as he suggested, watching in disbelief as he finished his redfish and then glanced covetously across the table at her untouched portion.

"Be my guest," she said sourly. She looked on as he devoured her fish, then patted his lips neatly with his napkin.

"Have a roll," he said, pushing the basket of bread toward her.

"Is it safe?" she asked. "Not baked with chili pepper, are they?"

"You're very suspicious," he said, wagging his finger at her.

"Occupational hazard," she replied. She took a roll and buttered it, moving her arm as the waiter removed their empty plates and replaced them with bowls of a steaming chowder. She surveyed the new arrival with a gimlet eye.

"It's all right," Landry said. "You'll like this."

"You expect me to listen to you after the last course?" Morgan demanded.

"I was just teasing you a little," Landry replied. "I had no intention of letting you leave here still hungry. The redfish takes a little working up to, but the gumbo is geared to popular taste."

"Whatever that means," Morgan grumbled, picking up her spoon. She sampled it and discovered that he was right; it was delicious.

"Well?" he said expectantly.

"It's wonderful," she admitted. "But don't think I'm forgetting the redfish. I'll get you back for that sometime."

"I'll look forward to it," Landry replied, with a smile that made Morgan's face grow warm. She became very interested in her food.

"More wine?" he asked.

Morgan shook her head. She had already imbibed enough to be eating aspirins like candy in the morning.

"I'm glad you like the gumbo," he said. "For a moment there I thought I was going to have to send out for pizza."

"That would have been fine with me. I have very pedestrian tastes."

"I thought women like you patronized the best restaurants," he said, regarding her quizzically.

"Women like me?" Morgan said, her spoon poised in midair.

"Professional women, urbane," Landry explained.

"When I'm on a case, take-out hamburgers at one in the morning is more like it," Morgan said. "And I'm usually on a case."

"I can't believe you have no social life," Landry said, watching her closely.

"I wouldn't say that," Morgan hedged, her tone mild.

"What would you say?" he pressed.

Morgan played with her silverware. She had known this man only a couple of days, spent less than four hours with him, and yet here he was asking personal, probing questions of her. Even more amazing was that she wanted to answer him, she wanted to tell him all about her, just as much as he wanted to know.

"I'd say," she answered slowly, "that right now I'm having a good time, the best time I've had in a long while. Is that enough?"

"That's enough," he conceded. "For right now."

"Beau," she began.

"Oh, good," he said dryly. "You're calling me 'Beau.'"

"That's your name."

"It was my name yesterday, and then you were calling me 'Mr. Landry,'" he pointed out to her.

"Beau," she said firmly.

"Yes?" He made the word into two syllables.

"About the deposition."

He held up a hand to forestall her. "You promised."

Morgan subsided. "Oh, all right."

The waiter cleared the plates and presented them with fluted silver champagne goblets filled with what looked like green ice cream.

"What's this?" Morgan asked.

"To cleanse the palate, *madame*," the waiter replied in an accent similar to Pete's.

"Okay," Morgan said, and looked at Landry.

"Mint julep sherbet," he said.

"That sounds intriguing," she said. She took a bite and raised her brows in approval.

"See," Landry said, "I told you the redfish was a red herring."

She groaned at the terrible joke, and he grinned.

"Is this what the drink tastes like?" she asked as the melting sherbet cooled her mouth.

"What drink?"

"A mint julep."

"Would you like one?" he asked, already signaling for the captain.

"No, no," Morgan said, grabbing for his hand. His generosity was instantaneous and overwhelming. It unnerved her.

He refused to release her fingers, twining them with his. When she tugged, he held her fast.

"Will you take the boat trip with me?" he asked, holding her eyes with his.

"Beau, I really don't think..." she began.

"Then don't think. Ignore all those Philadelphia rules for a minute and do what you want."

"Your connection with this case—"

He cut her off. "Forget it. Forget how we met and say yes."

Morgan hesitated.

"I have you at a disadvantage," he reminded her. "I could arm-wrestle you to the ground right now."

"In front of all these sedate diners?" Morgan asked, smiling.

"*Chère*, this is Cajun country," Landry said. "These people have seen much more scandalous behavior at dinner; they wouldn't bat an eyelash."

"All right," Morgan said, and he released her hand immediately.

"That's settled," he said, satisfied.

Morgan sat back in her chair, amazed. He also knew enough to retreat once a victory was secured; she was beginning to understand how he had turned his fortunes around single-handedly.

The crab arrived and it was heavenly. Morgan looked around as they ate, noticing that the line behind the reservation desk remained as long as it had been when they were seated.

"This must be a very popular place," she commented to Landry, who was observing her enthusiasm for the crab with amusement.

"It's in all the guides with a five-star rating," he said, "and that brings in the trade over the summer. Fall and winter, it's mostly locals."

"How do you know Pete, the waiter?"

"We grew up together. His sister was in my class at school. He wanted to wait on us himself, but the table I asked for wasn't in his section. They're very territorial, you know; repeat customers request the same service."

"Are you a repeat customer?" Morgan asked, putting down her fork. The crab was very rich and cloyed quickly.

"I come here when I want to give a lady a fine meal," he said.

"Oh. Does that mean you come here often?" Morgan asked ingenuously.

He laughed. "Often enough, *chère*. Don't interrogate me with those district attorney eyes. Finish your crab."

"I can't eat any more of it."

"Dessert, then?"

She shook her head.

"You must try the pralines in cream, or the pecan pie."

"I couldn't."

"You'll have some of mine, then," he said. He got the waiter and ordered dessert for himself, with two plates, and coffee.

"Is it time yet?" Morgan asked archly as a busboy cleared the table and brought complimentary candied fruit and ginger cookies.

"Go ahead," he said, his smile fading. He popped a slice of crystallized apricot into his mouth and sat waiting tensely, his good mood dispelled.

Morgan reached into her bag and brought out the papers she'd prepared, sorry that she had to remind him of the business aspect of the evening. She felt as if she were making him pay for her company, but then reminded herself that this plan was his idea.

"Now," she said, falling at once into the pleasant but distant attitude that came naturally to her when dealing with clients. "You do understand that you will be under penalty of perjury when answering these questions, just as if you were sworn in on the witness stand in court?"

"I understand," he said shortly.

"And you do understand that perjury is a knowing lie, a punishable offense in the jurisdiction, which is Pennsylvania, the state where TransAmerica does business, and that Sunlite and the plaintiffs have consented to this jurisdiction?"

"I understand all of that," he said impatiently. "Just get on with it."

"Now you are Beauregarde Justus Landry, owner and president of Landry Associates, doing business in the state of Louisiana at 182 Juniper Street, New Orleans?"

Landry looked at the ceiling. "You know who I am."

"Just answer the question."

"Yes." His reply was curt. Morgan noted it.

"And you are familiar with the circumstances of the suit named herein, Morales et al versus Sunlite Petroleum?" she asked.

"Yes." He was now staring over her shoulder, his eyes blank.

Morgan tried to make it painless, abbreviating the questions where possible, taking down the information as quickly as she could. His temper shortened with each inquiry, and by the time she was finished his mouth was a thin line. The dessert had arrived while they were talking, and it sat untouched on the table, the coffee growing cold beside it. The atmosphere was equally chilly.

"Could we have some fresh coffee?" Landry said tersely to the waiter, who was hovering, waiting to clear the table.

Morgan put the deposition in her purse. She would review it in detail later, but the upshot of it was that Landry had personally observed several incidences of what would constitute legal negligence, that is, negligent practices also in violation of local statutes. If Sunlite had behaved in a manner dangerous to its employees, but still within the law, the oil workers would have no case. Sunlite was held only to the standard of the law, no matter how lenient the law happened to be. But according to Landry, who was prepared to say the same in court, Sunlite's illegal practices had led directly to the deaths in question. So Sunlite was in big trouble—if he was telling the truth. Morgan looked across the table at him. Was he?

"All through, Counselor?" he said sarcastically.

"For the moment."

"Oh, there's more?"

"Possibly."

"So I'm not off the hook yet?"

She didn't answer.

"What's the matter?" Landry said. "You had enough to say a moment ago."

"You knew that I had to do my job," Morgan said quietly.

"Of course. You made it very clear that your, uh, job, was the only reason you agreed to go out with me."

"That's not fair," Morgan answered. "We're seeing one another again tomorrow."

"Have to keep the subject in a cooperative mood," Landry replied. "Might need him again; you just said so."

"That had nothing to do with it, and you're not going to make me feel as if I should be apologizing to you," Morgan said sharply. "I didn't spring that deposition on you tonight. You understood the situation when you asked me here."

They stared at one another as the waiter brought a second set of cups and a new pot of coffee. If he noticed the arctic air mass hovering over the table he pretended to be oblivious. Landry waited for him to leave and then sighed, looking away from Morgan.

"I suppose I was hoping that you would change your mind," he said softly.

"How could I change my mind? It's my duty to represent my client to the best of my ability. Did you really think you could finesse me into neglecting it?"

"I wasn't trying to 'finesse' you into anything," he said heatedly. "I was just hoping that...."

"What?" Morgan said.

He looked at her, then down. "Never mind. Drink your coffee, it doesn't matter."

But it did matter. The unresolved issue lingered between them as he paid the check and they went out into the reception area, where a waiting valet got his car.

It was a miserable drive back to the hotel. Landry put a jazz cassette on the stereo as soon as they left New Orleans. The music created a barrier he didn't attempt to bridge with conversation until he had pulled into a parking space near the hotel in Bienville.

"I'll go up with you," he said, and got out of the car.

"That isn't necessary," Morgan replied.

He wasn't listening. He opened her door and stood aside as she got out, then followed her in silence into the hotel and through the lobby to the elevators.

"I'll be fine from here," she said.

He didn't even look at her, merely hit the call button with his fist and then stared at the metal doors until they popped open. He stepped into the elevator behind her when she got on.

"Are you going to follow me to my room?" she asked indignantly.

"I'm going to walk you to your door," he replied between clenched teeth. Morgan decided not to challenge this statement, and allowed him to trail her down the carpeted hallway until they were standing outside her room.

"This is it," Morgan said briskly. "Good night." She removed the hotel key from her purse.

Landry took her by the shoulders and spun her around to face him.

"Look," he said fiercely, "I can't leave you this way. I won't."

"Beau," she said reasonably, "I'm not going to hold you to the commitment for tomorrow night. I realize this is ending uncomfortably and—"

She never finished the sentence. He bent his head quickly and kissed her, stunning her with his swiftness. But surprise soon changed to submission as she gave herself to his embrace. Her fingers relaxed and the room key fell to the floor.

His mouth was softer than she would have guessed, tasting of wine. When he saw that she wouldn't resist, one arm enclosed her, drawing her into the curve of his body. With his other hand he held her steady, sinking his fingers into the wealth of hair at the back of her neck.

Morgan's head fell back, and she wound her arms around his waist. He was muscular, hard; clothing made him look leaner than he was, disguising the results of years spent in physical labor. He smelled wonderful, clean and masculine, a combination of soap and starch and a subtle, tantalizing musk. When he lifted his mouth from hers, Morgan's eyes opened slowly.

He was watching her, his arms still around her. As she stared up at him, he lifted one hand and ran his knuckles along the side of her neck.

"Come," he whispered. "Come back to me."

She swayed toward him, her eyes closing again instinctively. He kissed her once more, but lightly, and then let her go, bending to pick up her key.

"I think you dropped this," he said, handing it to her.

Morgan took it mechanically.

"I'll pick you up here tomorrow night at eight," he said quietly. "All right?"

Morgan nodded, mute.

"Good night, *chère*," he said. He set off down the hall and she watched him until he had turned the corner for the elevators. Then she unlocked her door with a shaking hand and let herself into her room.

Three

Morgan awoke the next morning to the expected headache and a vague, dreamlike memory of her parting with Landry the previous night. Had he really kissed her with such passion? And had she really responded the same way? It seemed like a fantasy in the bright morning sunlight, but she had the faint marks of his fingers on her upper arms to prove that it was true. Her pale, lightly freckled skin always bruised as easily as a peach. Landry's hand had left an imprint like a brand.

She took two aspirins and a shower, and called down to room service for a pot of coffee when she emerged from the bathroom. She was just belting her terry robe when her bedside telephone rang.

"Hello?" she said tentatively, putting one hand to her forehead.

"Good morning, kiddo, it's the long arm of Philly," Julie's cheerful voice sang.

"Oh, hi," Morgan replied. Julie was her assistant at TA, a recent law school graduate clerking in the litigation department until she could take the bar exam in the fall.

"Do I detect a certain lack of enthusiasm in that greeting?" Julie inquired.

"Headache," Morgan explained.

"Ah-ha. Hitting the booze again?" It was a standard joke at work that Morgan, who drank the least, suffered the most from it.

"Just a glass of wine, but it was enough."

"And exactly why were you chugging vino when you're supposed to be working on a case?"

"I went to dinner with Beau Landry and . . . oh, it's a long story."

There was a silence. Then, "You went to dinner with the chief witness against Sunlite?"

"I had to get his deposition."

"Let me guess. You deposed him in the restaurant."

"That's right."

There was another silence. Then, "Morgan, Jerry is not going to like this."

"Jerry" was Jeremiah Sinclair, the litigation chief at TA. His vocabulary consisted of two phrases: "No, no" and "No, absolutely not."

"Jerry won't know unless you tell him, Julie," Morgan responded wearily.

"Well of course I'm not going to tell him," Julie said indignantly, "but I don't want to be around if he finds out about it. You know his opinion concerning social interaction with company contacts."

"I have a date with Landry tonight," Morgan said, deciding to confide it all. Well, almost all.

"Morgan!" Julie's voice became a squeak.

"There's nothing unethical about what I'm doing," Morgan said, to convince herself as well as her friend. "I'm not jeopardizing the case, in fact I'm helping it. We needed that deposition, and I had to show some creativity to get it. Landry was being uncooperative. And if I want to see him now, that's my business. Jerry's attitude is his own, not the company's." So there.

"I know that, you don't have to sell me," Julie replied, sounding irritated. "But Jerry is your—our—boss."

"That doesn't mean he's God. What I do on my own time doesn't concern him."

"Well, I see we're going to be stubborn about this," Julie commented. "I hope Landry is worth it."

"I don't know if he is or not, but I'm not going to let Jerry Sinclair's narrow-minded views control my life," Morgan said firmly.

"Yeah, and I can imagine why," Julie replied. "I saw Landry's picture, remember?"

"You did?"

"Sure. When I was doing the prelim on the case for you."

"I don't remember that."

"I went through the press clippings about the oil field accident. I scanned them for potential witnesses before the file was sent on to Jerry's office."

"Oh, that's right."

"Mr. Landry's pretty cute, as I recall. Even in grainy newsprint he was memorable."

"He's memorable, all right," Morgan said thoughtfully.

"Which is why you're risking the wrath of the formidable Jeremiah Sinclair by snuggling up to him."

"Oh, for heaven's sake, Julie, I'm not snuggling up to him," Morgan said, exasperated. "What a thing to say."

"Then what are you doing?" Julie asked, interested.

Morgan tapped her foot, curling the telephone wire in her hands as she sat on the bed. "I accepted one date with him, that's all."

"What was last night?"

"That was business." Morgan mentally edited out the kiss; Julie was whipped up enough already.

"Dinner, with wine?" Julie inquired. "My business meetings usually involve stale cigarette smoke and flat, warm colas. A tuna fish sandwich if I'm lucky. Sounds to me like this guy is giving you a rush."

"I don't know about that. He keeps making rotten cracks about lawyers."

"Oh, one of those."

"He thinks we're all crooks."

"Which is why he keeps asking you out."

"Look, Julie, I can't explain it, I'm having a little trouble with it myself. He's somewhat...contradictory."

"Sounds like it." Papers rattled in the background, and then Julie said, "I hate to bring up an unpleasant subject, namely work, but what was the gist of Landry's deposition? Jerry wants to know."

"Landry says he directly observed legal negligence, and he enumerated several instances for me, with details and dates."

"Oh-oh. Not so good for our side."

"That's about the size of it. I'll express mail a copy of the deposition now if Jerry wants to see it, but I was going to wait until I did a little more groundwork before sending it to you. I'm interviewing Landry's crew chief today, two of the staff engineers on Friday, some others later on.''

"Better wait and send it all together. When are you seeing the plaintiff families?''

Morgan sighed. "I'm leaving them for last. Hopefully I'll have enough material by then and I won't have to hit them too hard.''

"I gather you're not looking forward to that,'' Julie said sympathetically.

"It won't be my favorite task,'' Morgan admitted.

"You'd like to see them recover, wouldn't you?''

"I'd like to see this whole thing end,'' Morgan replied. "I hate these tough ones, where you wind up with the sneaking feeling that you're representing the wrong client.''

"Landry must have been pretty convincing.''

"He was. If he gets on the witness stand, the jury will hand Sunlite over to the plaintiffs on a platter. Garnished with parsley.''

"Then don't give him the chance to talk. Settle.''

"I'll wait to see what the rest of the players have to say. I'll let you know how it goes. Tell Jerry to keep his shirt on.''

"That will be a pleasure. Who wants to see Jerry with his shirt off?''

"Is he estimating my expenses already?'' Morgan asked, grinning.

"You betcha. Complaining about the hotel prices. Too high.''

"How does he know? I haven't sent in one voucher yet.''

"He saw the brochure and had a fit. Marble floors, Oriental rugs. That calculator in his head started clicking right away.''

"Yeah, well if he thinks he's sending me to another cockroach heaven like that place in Minneapolis, he's crazy."

"He loved it. It was cheap."

"It was dangerous. There were insects the size of golden retrievers scampering across the floors. The dining room served Legionnaires' disease with the entrées. I would have reported it to the board of health except I didn't want to miss the el cheapo 3:00 a.m. flight Jerry had so thoughtfully booked."

"He's a prince," Julie agreed.

"Thank God he was too busy to come with me this time. If I had to endure another experience like Minneapolis I think I would have shot him."

Morgan heard a buzzer go off in the background, and Julie said, "Duty calls. I'll be in touch. Take it easy, and don't worry about the home front. I'm on top of everything here."

"Thanks a lot, Julie."

"Bye-bye."

"Goodbye."

Morgan hung up the phone and went to the mirror to comb out her wet hair. The banging in her head had subsided somewhat, and she consulted her notes on the man she was to see that morning. His name was Pierre Darriet, and he had been working for Landry for six years as crew boss for the oil rigs. She was meeting him downstairs in the hotel conference room at ten.

Her coffee arrived, and she sipped it as she dressed, wondering if she should heed Julie's words of warning. Her desire to continue seeing Landry wasn't just defiance of an unreasonable, overbearing boss, despite the picture she had painted for Julie. She simply couldn't resist Landry; this was the first time she had ever been involved with a participant in a case. Honesty compelled her to admit, if only to herself, that the thought did make her uncomfortable.

She went downstairs early and was sitting by herself at the oval conference table when Darriet entered. She stood to offer her hand.

"Mr. Darriet, thank you for coming," she said. "I'm Attorney Taylor."

He nodded, pumping her hand briefly, and then stood uneasily next to a chair, unwilling to sit until she did. He was a handsome man in his late forties, with deep laugh lines around his eyes and a few threads of gray at his temples.

"Please, sit down," Morgan said, pulling out her own chair and easing into it. He obeyed, watching her warily.

"Now, Mr. Darriet," Morgan began.

"Call me Pete," he said, wiping his palms on the thighs of his jeans. He was dressed for work and had obviously come from the field to meet her. His boots were caked with drying mud.

"All right, Pete. Now you understand that I'm here to ask you questions about the accident that happened last September on the Sunlite rig at the Wentworth tract." Wentworth had been the original owner of the land, and it was still known by that name.

He nodded again. Morgan explained to him the formalities of the proceeding and his obligation to tell the truth, exactly as she had outlined the situation to Landry in the restaurant. Darriet said nothing, his blue eyes on her face.

"First of all, Pete, I have to ask you if Mr. Landry, or anyone else, has attempted to influence you in what you are about to say."

"Pardon?" Pete said, and Morgan winced at her lack of insight. His accent indicated that he was bilingual, and she would bet that French was his first language. She'd better can the legalese and speak plainly.

"Has your boss talked to you about this?" Morgan revised her question.

Pete shrugged. "He say to tell what I saw."

"Has anyone else talked to you about this?"

He shook his head.

"All right." Morgan made a note. Wishing desperately that she could speak French, she said, "While you were working on the Wentworth site, did you see anything dangerous going on?"

"Dangerous," he said. He pronounced it "dahnjereuse."

"Something Sunlite was doing, or not doing, that made the place unsafe for the workers."

Pete nodded vigorously. "They no inspect the rig."

"They didn't inspect the rig," Morgan repeated, writing it down. Landry had said the same thing. "How often did the inspectors come?"

Pete waved his hand. "Oh, from the state, twice a year. But the company know that's not enough, must be checked once a month, once every six weeks by their own people."

"I see," Morgan said, scribbling furiously. "I know that the statute, the law, requires only a bi-yearly inspection, but you maintain it is standard practice within the industry to keep a closer watch on the rig."

"But of course," Pete said, as if she were an idiot. "I don't care what the law say, Sunlite know better. They cut back, they lay off the inspectors to save money, understand?"

"I understand," Morgan replied. She understood only too well, but what he was saying wasn't going to help the oil workers' families, it was going to help Sunlite. The company was held only to the standard of the law. It didn't matter that everyone knew the rig should be inspected more frequently. As long as Sunlite did it twice a year, they were covered. Sunlite had obviously been walking a fine line between what was legal and what was safe.

Morgan questioned Pete in further detail to try to pinpoint actual code violations, but Pete was not as familiar with the law as his boss and could only talk in vague generalities about wires left ungrounded and hoists with loose springs. Morgan would have to do some further research into the local codes to determine whether this was a gray area where Sunlite might win if they took it to court, or whether Landry was right, and Sunlite didn't have a chance.

She finished with Pete and sat staring at her papers, hoping that she wasn't immersed up to her eyeballs in what her old torts professor had referred to as a "slipshod workmanship" case. In such situations the law was not as stringent as it should be, either because of a lax legislature or lobbying on the part of the industry in question, and as a result the industry literally got away with murder. Thus, electricians were allowed to use aluminum wire in buildings, even though it had been proven that copper wire was ten times less likely to catch fire. And when a house burned down and took a family of five with it, the builder pointed to the law and washed his hands of blame.

But Landry seemed to be sure that Sunlite had done more than take advantage of a lenient code; he had named dates and places and actual violations of the law.

Yet when she had mentioned these to Pete, he had shrugged and said it was certainly possible, even likely, but he didn't know for sure.

Morgan rubbed the frown line between her brows. She didn't like the picture that was emerging. This was going to be a long haul: hard work and conflicting testimony and a client for which she had little sympathy. This was the aspect of her profession that she enjoyed the least—representing somebody to the best of her ability, because that was her job, when her heart was lined up with the other side.

One thing was certain. She didn't want to be confused by a developing personal relationship with Beau Landry while trying to evaluate this case. She would leave a message at his office saying that she wouldn't be able to see him that evening. Feeling extremely disappointed, but very virtuous, she went back to her room to make the call.

Morgan spent the day at the Tulane law school library doing research. When she got back to the hotel at four, the message light on her telephone was blinking.

Morgan checked with the desk clerk and discovered that Mr. Landry had called four times. Oh, boy. It was clear that he wasn't going to go away quietly.

She was undressing to take her second shower of the day when the telephone rang. Morgan picked up the receiver deliberately.

"Hello?"

"What's this about your canceling our date?" Landry demanded without preliminaries.

"Hello, Beau."

"Well, at least you know who it is," he said sarcastically.

"Look, Beau, I don't want to hurt your feelings...."

"You have," he said crisply.

Morgan closed her eyes. "I just think it's a bad idea for us to carry this any further."

"You thought it was a good idea last night."

"No, I didn't. You just sort of, well, overwhelmed me."

There was a pause. Then, "Let me get this straight. You can't say no to me when I'm with you, but the minute I leave, you start thinking about your Hippocratic oath or something, am I right?"

"That's doctors," she said automatically.

"Don't dodge the question. Am I right?"

Morgan didn't answer.

He interpreted her silence as assent. "So, as I understand it," he went on reasonably, "the immediate problem is that I'm not there."

"What?" Morgan said, alarmed.

"I'm calling from the lobby. I'll be right up."

"Wait a minute!" Morgan said urgently, but the line had gone dead. She hung up with excessive force. Damn him, he was going to appear on her threshold at any second and she was standing around in her underwear. She raced to the bathroom and shrugged into her robe just as he began pounding on her door. He must have raced up the steps two at a time.

"Morgan, let me in," he called.

She hesitated, debating how to handle him.

"I'm not leaving," he warned her. "You have to come out sometime, and when you do, I'll be here."

Morgan briefly considered testing that contention by letting him spend the night in the hall, but her desire to have him shut up and stop creating a scene won out over her indignation. She yanked open the door.

"Hi," he said calmly, as if he hadn't been yelling through the oak paneling two seconds earlier.

"What do you mean by carrying on like that in a public place?" she demanded furiously.

"Going to have me arrested, Counselor?" he asked, quirking one eyebrow at her.

"I should," she said darkly.

"Oh, don't be such a proper Philadelphia miss," he said, smiling. "Aren't you glad to see me?"

"No."

"Liar," he said equably.

"Go away."

"You look awfully fetching in that shortie thing," he said. "What is it?"

"It's a bathrobe. Goodbye," Morgan responded, and swung the door inward.

He stuck his foot in the jamb. "Let me in."

"I will not."

"Aw, come on. I just want to talk to you for a few minutes."

Morgan stared at him. He was wearing a short-sleeved, yellow cotton shirt that emphasized his dark good looks. Was she really going to send this man away?

"All right," she said, stepping aside. "For a few minutes."

"That's all I'll need," he replied, striding past her.

"Such confidence," she said dryly, slamming the door.

He stopped before the easy chair by the window and said, "May I?"

"Oh, be my guest," Morgan said, gesturing expansively. She sat cautiously on the edge of the bed and watched as he settled comfortably into the chair, crossing his chino-clad legs at the ankle, exposing butter-soft leather moccasins.

"So what's the story?" he inquired directly. "Got cold feet?"

He really could be irritating. She regarded him frostily.

"Afraid of losing your job?"

"This may come as a shock to you, Mr. Landry..."

He rolled his eyes. "I've been demoted to Mr. Landry again," he observed darkly.

"...but some of us actually have professional ethics," Morgan finished.

"Where were they when you were kissing me last night?" he asked.

Morgan stood. "Get out," she said, heading for the door.

He jumped up, blocking her path. "Morgan, wait, I'm sorry," he said hastily.

She glared at him.

"Look," he said placatingly, holding out his hands, "I shouldn't have said that. But you're driving me crazy. I thought we had a good time last night."

She dropped her eyes.

"Well, at least I did," he went on. He put his palms on her shoulders lightly, and she allowed them to remain. "I kissed you," he said softly. "You kissed me back."

Morgan said nothing.

"Didn't you?" he murmured.

"Yes," she whispered.

"Kiss me again," he urged quietly, his face inches away.

Morgan's lips parted. Her eyes were closing, his mouth about to touch hers, when she jumped back, her hands going to her head.

"What am I doing?" she moaned. "Am I losing my mind? You come storming in here, making a terrible scene, pulling these cornball tactics out of a bad movie, and I'm *falling* for them. What is wrong with me? I don't even know you!''

"Take it easy," he said, as if dealing with a recalcitrant mental patient. "Take it easy."

"I will not take it easy. Get out of my room this instant before I, before I..." She couldn't think of anything bad enough to say.

"Are you angry with me, or yourself?" he asked quietly.

"Oh, shut up. I've had enough of your cute one-liners. You're confusing me and upsetting me and I won't have it. This case is important to my career. It's the first major assignment I've been permitted to handle alone, and I'm not going to let you or anyone else louse it up for me."

He put his hands behind his back, as if demonstrating that he wasn't about to molest her. "I'm not trying to louse up your career, woman, all I want is a date," he said, making light of her reaction.

"That's not all you want," she said wisely, her eyes narrowing.

"Two dates?" he suggested, and relaxed when she had to smile.

"There, that's better," he said. "So are we still on for tonight?"

She shook her head admiringly. "You don't give up, do you?"

"Not with something I really want."

Morgan bit her lip.

"You want to go, don't you?" he said softly.

"Unlike you, Beau," Morgan replied tiredly, "my life is not always ruled by what I *want*."

"Duty first, eh?" he said.

Morgan looked at him.

"What are you, a marine?" he said, turning away disgustedly.

"Beau, it's complicated."

He whirled to face her again. "No, it's simple. Come with me. Be with me. Forget everything else for tonight." He saw her hesitation and pressed. "Will you?"

She bent her head, then nodded.

"I'll pick you up at seven-thirty," he said hastily, before she could change her mind. He angled toward the door.

"Beau," she called after him.

"Seven-thirty," he repeated, and left, pulling the door closed after him.

Morgan sank into the chair he had vacated, feeling drained, as if she had lost a crucial battle. Her mind raced for several minutes, and then she got up to drag the phone from the nightstand back to her seat. She dialed the hotel operator and placed a long-distance call, her expression preoccupied.

"Hello?" Julie's voice on the other end was brisk.

"Julie, it's me," Morgan said. "I'm glad you're still there. I was afraid I'd get the service."

"Morgan. Didn't I just talk to you this morning?"

"Yes, but I need your advice on something."

"What is it?" Julie's tone was alert now, expectant.

"What kind of a mood is Jerry in?"

"Are you kidding? What kind of a mood is he ever in? Spitting nails."

"I was afraid you were going to say that," Morgan observed glumly.

"Why?"

"I don't suppose there's any chance he'd let me turn this assignment over to somebody else?" Morgan asked, closing one eye, wincing.

"What!" Julie's voice was squeaking again. "Morgan, what the hell is going on down there?"

"Well . . ." Morgan said inadequately.

"You begged for that assignment! You begged to take it on alone."

"Please don't remind me," Morgan mumbled.

"Is it Landry? What's he doing?"

"What isn't he doing?"

"Tell me."

Morgan took a deep breath. "I feel I shouldn't be seeing him while I'm on this case, but I can't seem to stop seeing him, so I thought the only thing to do would be to give up the case."

"I see." Julie sighed heavily. "If I tell Jerry this he's going to hang you from the TA flagpole when you get back. Not to mention what he's going to do to me when I deliver the bulletin. Remember those Greeks who used to execute the messengers who brought them bad news?"

"We could tell him I got sick," Morgan volunteered weakly.

Julie thought that over for a moment. "He might buy that." She paused. "I know! I'll tell him that you're not feeling well, and the case is more complex than you thought, and you need me to come down there and help you!"

"Julie," Morgan said cautiously.

"No, it's perfect, don't you see? Bill Travers can take over for me here, and I'm sure you really could use a hand. What do you say?"

"Jerry won't pay for another room."

"We'll share."

"Plane fare."

"I'll fly orange crate airlines, I don't care. Come on, let me try. You sound like you could certainly use a friend."

"I could," Morgan admitted.

"I'll call you back tomorrow," Julie said. "And until then, keep the faith."

"I'll try." Morgan hung up, feeling as though she had spent the whole day on the phone. Then she stood, heading for the bathroom to take her shower.

Four

Morgan dressed in cotton twill slacks with a sleeveless blouse and wore a pair of canvas espadrilles for comfort. She didn't know what was appropriate for a Mississippi cruise, but it was still very hot and she didn't want to make an enemy of the weather. She put her hair in a ponytail to keep it off her neck, and then had second thoughts when she glanced in the mirror. The total effect was to make her appear about sixteen, like Debbie Reynolds in *Susan Slept Here*. She decided to let it go. Landry was currently progressing at the speed of light; if she looked underage it might slow him down a little.

Morgan sat cross-legged on the bed and contemplated her life. It had all gone more or less according to plan until she'd arrived in Louisiana. She'd never imagined that meeting Beau Landry would throw everything into chaos. She felt like a derailed freight train.

It was clear that he would not go away, and it was also clear that she didn't want him to. How she was going to manage both him and Sunlite was another matter, but for this evening she was going to worry about one thing: the man. The case would have to wait.

It was seven-twenty. To forestall another dramatic appearance at her door, Morgan decided to go down to the lobby. She was sitting on one of the needlepoint sofas when Landry entered.

She saw him before he saw her. He spoke to the doorman in friendly fashion and strolled through the entrance, his hands in his pockets. He was wearing jeans with a loose cotton shirt in pale blue. He looked cool and unruffled, and Morgan felt a momentary surge of anger. How dare he look so unaffected when she felt as jumpy as a squirrel? The conclusion that she didn't want to come to was that he dazzled impressionable ladies like herself all the time, going from one to the other with casual aplomb. Was this "rush," as Julie described it, going to last just as long as her visit to New Orleans, with him moving on to a new challenge when she'd gone back home?

Landry caught sight of her and smiled, his teeth flashing white in his tanned face. Morgan got up and went toward him.

"Hi," he said, looking her over. "Cute outfit. Kind of like Girl Scouts. Are we going camping?"

"Not if I can help it," she said meaningfully, and he laughed.

"Relax, *chère*, you look nervous."

"Do I?" Morgan asked, trying not to look nervous.

"You look like you're asking yourself, 'Should I be getting on a boat with this man?' "

"Should I?"

"Absolutely. There were a few inland pirates in the Landry clan, but they've been dead for hundreds of years. I'm perfectly safe."

"I doubt that."

He grinned and took her hand. He swung it between them as they walked through the lobby.

"Do you really have pirate ancestors?" Morgan asked.

"So the story goes." They passed through the doors to the outside, where the weather was still sticky but cooling with nightfall. "The name was spelled L-a-n-d-r-e-e in those days, and supposedly the Landrees disappeared into the bayous with their ill-gotten gains. And the requisite captured maidens. Can you believe it?"

"I believe it," Morgan said fervently.

He cast her a sidelong glance. "Oh, so it's obvious I come from dangerous stock?"

"Pirates are dangerous."

He winked. "Bear that in mind." He handed her into his car, tipping the attendant who held the door. When he got in beside her, she said, "Where are we going?"

"To the boat. Pay attention to the program."

"No, I mean right now. Isn't the river just behind us? We could walk there."

"I'm driving to the levee. The boat is tied up there."

"You really do have levees," she said, smiling. "Somehow I thought they only existed in songs."

"'Drove my chevy to the levee but the levee was dry,'" he sang softly.

She giggled. "That's right."

"'Down on the levee, with Ephraim and Sammy, it's a treat to beat your feet on the Mississippi mud,'" he caroled, changing tune, throwing his head back like Al Jolson.

"You must know them all," Morgan said, smiling.

"Well, the river kind of dominates the scene down here," he admitted. "If it were three thousand years ago, we'd be like the Egyptians worshipping the Nile."

"Did you always live here?"

He nodded. "Always. I get itchy when I'm too far away from that water, as if it's a person I miss. I like to be able to see it." He turned into an alley running between two dockside buildings and parked the car in a slot marked Tesreau.

"Who's Tesreau?" Morgan asked as they got out. The river smell assaulted her, much stronger than it had been in the restaurant, green and brown and earthy. Darkness gathered, contributing to the primeval atmosphere.

"My friend."

"Where will he park?"

"He isn't coming."

Morgan stopped walking. "Then who's running the boat?"

"I am," Landry responded casually. "I have a river pilot's license. I've taken small craft all the way up to St. Louis." He guided her around the car and onto the wooden gangway of a miniature two-deck cruiser, complete with paddle wheel, exactly as advertised.

"This isn't what I pictured," Morgan said, following him into the pilot's cabin and looking out over the water. "I thought you could see the tide marks on the levee."

"New Orleans is just at sea level," Landry explained. "It used to be below it, and the town was drained for habitation. You're thinking of Vicksburg, Natchez, the river towns north of us. At Vicksburg when the river is low you can walk up the cement levee for a quarter of a mile. When it's at its highest, the levee is all covered right up to the street. You can jump off the boat directly onto the road.''

"I've heard that." But she couldn't picture it.

"Vicksburg is on a bluff. During the big floods earlier in the century a good part of the town was destroyed. They finally built that cement levee to hold the water back." He leaned against the pilot's wheel, his arms folded.

"A terrible battle was fought there," Morgan said softly.

"In high summer, too. At one point they called a recess just to bury the dead. The bodies were rotting in the field from the heat."

Morgan shuddered. "How awful."

"You should go to see the battlefield," he said, "it's an historic park now. I'll take you if you want. You'd like the Alabama monument. It's very poetic, beautiful."

"Why do you think I'd like that one in particular?" Morgan asked.

"It's a monument to the Confederate women, the sacrifices they made for the South."

"Oh."

"I wish you could see Natchez, too," he went on. "Metal stairs run up the levee from the water right to the road above. The number of stairs you have to climb depends on the water level when you get there."

"That'll keep you in shape," Morgan said dryly. "If you can't make it up the stairs you're stuck on the boat."

"You'll never have that problem, slim," he said. He touched her cheek. "Just wait here," he added. "I've got to cast off the lines, get clearance to move out of the slip. I'll be right back."

Morgan busied herself studying the instrument panel while he was gone. A glass shield rose above it to enclose the cabin. She was examining the huge wooden wheel, its surface pitted and stained, the varnish worn off from the grip of many fingers, when he returned.

"All set," he informed her. He stood next to her and flipped a couple of switches on the oak panel. The diesel engine rumbled to life beneath their feet.

"That's . . . loud," Morgan said uneasily.

"I'll adjust it," he said, smiling, "it'll calm down in a minute." He played with more dials and then stood at the wheel, one hand resting on its crossbar. The motor subsided obediently. Morgan looked at the levee and realized that Landry's car was receding.

"We're moving!" she crowed delightedly.

"That's right," he agreed. "Have a little faith in the pilot."

She stood at his shoulder and watched as he guided the boat away from the bank and out into the river. She said nothing, observing his concentration. Several minutes went by, as they passed all manner of craft at dock and in the water, before he spoke to her.

"There we go," he said. "All set."

"Are we out of New Orleans?" Morgan asked. It didn't look it. Buildings and homes, their lights strung along the shore like beads, still crowded the riverbank.

"No, it goes on for miles. We just cleared the docking limits. It will be a while before we hit the open river."

"What's out there?" Morgan asked.

"Trees," he said dryly. "Lots of trees."

"No houses?"

"Not at the water level. That changes so much from flooding they'd be buried half the year. Most of the trees you see tonight will be under water next spring."

"Then where are the plantations?" Morgan demanded, imbued with the lore of the Old South.

"Inland a couple of miles. Most times you have to reach them by an estuary, a small stream that leads down to the main water."

"Oh," Morgan said, disappointed.

He looked at her, amused. "What's the matter? Expected to see Tara, complete with pillared mansion and Vivien Leigh in a green dress, as you floated by?"

"Don't make fun of me," Morgan said, feigning annoyance.

"So ignorant, you Northerners," he said teasingly. "Morgan, this is the largest river in North America. Do you realize what happens when it rises? The whole complexion of life changes. A hundred years ago it controlled agriculture, warfare—an entire society. Modern life has altered that somewhat, of course, but the power is still there, you can always feel it."

"The Father of Waters," Morgan murmured.

"You bet," he said emphatically.

They fell silent as the boat picked up speed, leaving New Orleans behind in the darkness. Landry kept the boat to one side, allowing the larger craft to use the deep channel in the middle of the river. They passed a great many slow-moving barges and some pleasure boats, brightly lit. The sound of music and laughter drifted to them over the water. Finally the traffic thinned, and they seemed to be alone, surrounded by the whispering, murky water.

"I see what you meant about the trees," Morgan said at last. They crowded in on either side as the river widened—dark, irregular shapes against the night sky, which looked like an indigo velvet cloak scattered with diamond chips.

"What's our destination?" Morgan asked.

"St. Francisville," he said shortly. He put his arm around her and she leaned into his shoulder.

"I can't believe how big it is," she said softly. "You could almost think you were on the sea."

"Oh, the river is narrow here," he told her. "You should see it at St. Louis. It does look like an ocean."

"This dwarfs the Delaware completely," Morgan said. "At some points, where it separates New Jersey and Pennsylvania, near Trenton, you can wave to the people on the other side."

"How wide is it there?" Landry asked.

"About a mile, I guess."

"You could swim that."

"Maybe *you* could," Morgan said, laughing. "I couldn't."

He looked at her. "Can't swim?" he said. It obviously hadn't occurred to him. Everybody he knew was amphibious.

"Oh, I can swim a little. Enough to pass my high school gym class," Morgan replied. "But I don't think any mile-long treks are in my future."

He leaned forward, relieved, and examined the riverbank to his right. "Should be just about here," he said thoughtfully. His breath stirred the tendrils of loose hair at her temples.

"What?" Morgan asked, peering in the direction in which he was looking. All she could see was an endless mass of vegetation, almost indistinguishable from the horizon.

"There it is." He turned the wheel, and the boat moved obediently to the right, churning water in its wake. They edged over gradually for what seemed like a long time until he said, "We're out of the current now. Got to stick it here." He cut the motor and the boat idled, lifting gently in its own wake. He sprinted to drop the anchor and then returned, examining his instruments.

"Beau, what are we doing?"

"See the estuary?" he said, pointing. She looked and saw the overgrown shore, nothing more.

"We can swim in from here," he said.

She turned to look up at him. "I didn't bring a suit."

"You don't need a suit," he said, pulling his shirt over his head.

"I," Morgan said, emphasizing the first word, "need a suit."

"Your underwear will do fine," he said patiently, as if talking to a child. "I'll bet it covers more than a bikini."

"I don't wear bikinis," Morgan said stiffly. She watched as he discarded his shirt and reached for his belt. He was as brown as a chestnut all over, with long ropy muscles in his arms and a deep inverted vee of black hair running down his chest. She tried not to stare.

He was wearing brief jogging shorts under his jeans. He pulled off his shoes and then looked up at her.

"May I ask a question?" she said archly.

"Fire away."

"Maybe I missed something, some sort of explanation or clue, but all of this is moving a little too quickly for me. Why did we stop here, and why do we have to swim anywhere?"

"We stopped because the estuary that leads to Belle Isle is right over there. We had to anchor out a distance because it's too shallow for the boat closer in. We swim to the shore and then take the canoe up the estuary to the house. Or what's left of the house."

"Canoe?" Morgan said faintly. She cleared her throat. "Am I to understand that we are now going to paddle, in a canoe, upriver, through that . . . that *forest*, in the middle of the night, in our *underwear*?''

"I'll be doing the paddling," he said reasonably. "And you can swim in your clothes if you like."

"Beau, I am not going," she said firmly.

"Why not?"

"It doesn't strike you that this is a bit more than I bargained for? You said a boat trip, not a remake of *Deliverance*. The answer is no."

He studied her, his dark eyes hooded, unreadable in the faint glow from the cabin's overhead light. Then he nodded. "I get it."

She waited.

"You're afraid of me. You're afraid to go with me."

Morgan didn't answer.

"You think I brought you all the way out here to attack you?" he said.

"Beau . . ."

"Believe me, Morgan, if that were my intention, I wouldn't need these elaborate preparations to accomplish it. I wanted to share something with you, something important to me, and that's *all* I wanted." He looked away. "I'm going for a swim. You can stay here and wait. I'll be back in a few minutes and I'll take you home." With that he turned and, placing one hand on the boat's railing, vaulted over it into the water.

Morgan heard the splash below and ran to see him doing an expert crawl toward the shore. She watched until he clambered up on the riverbank, then she turned back into the boat, feeling upset and frustrated. She was sure her reaction to his plan wasn't unreasonable, but why did she regret it? She thought a moment, then stripped off her clothes with resignation. In seconds she wore nothing but her bra and panties. She hoisted herself to the rail and swung her feet over it into empty space. It was higher than she had thought, and she closed her eyes, holding her nose as she jumped.

The water was cold, a shock considering the air temperature, and she shot to the surface, shivering. The first thing she heard was Landry's voice.

"Morgan, are you all right?" he was calling. She could see him running toward the water.

"I'm fine," she shouted, and mustered her ten-year-old swimming lessons into an acceptable forward motion. He splashed into the shallows and grabbed her as she emerged from the water. His hands slid down her wet arms, and she felt their strength almost lifting her off the marshy river bottom.

"What the hell kind of a stunt was that?" he demanded.

She pulled away. "I decided to join you."

He stared at her. "I thought you fell overboard," he said.

Morgan stared back. "Beau, how could I fall overboard? The railing is four feet high."

"Well, I knew you didn't want to come with me."

She started to laugh, and he had to join in, ruefully. He let her go and walked back to the bank, dropping full length on an outcropping of gorse.

Morgan followed slowly and sat next to him.

"So," she said, "here we are."

"Yes, indeed," he said dryly.

"Thank you for bringing me."

He turned and stared at her. "What? A minute ago you were giving me a hard time about all this."

"The trip here wasn't what I was objecting to, and you know it."

He didn't answer for a moment, then sighed. "Look, you were right. I should have explained what I had in mind. I presumed too much. I really didn't mean to scare you."

"I wasn't scared of you, exactly."

"No?"

"Maybe of myself."

He let that pass. "Sometimes," he said, "when I have an idea, I just get carried away. I should have realized how it would look. I should have told you more." He shrugged. "It would be better to go by daylight anyway, safer. It's just so beautiful at night, I wanted you to see it. It seemed important, somehow." He shrugged. "I can't explain."

"You don't have to explain," Morgan said quietly. "I understand."

He turned his head to look at her fully, his wet hair glistening in the moonlight.

"It is beautiful," she added.

And it was. The water lapped softly at their feet, the breeze was light, redolent of the marsh plants growing at river's edge, and the moonlight bathed them in an amber glow. The sounds of the boat traffic in the channel were muted, distant, competing with the nearby calls of loons in the live oak trees. And over all of it lay a hush, almost reverential, made of the night air and the whispering water and the breath of the man beside her.

"Sometimes," Landry said quietly, "when I was a kid, I would sit by the water at night, and if it was calm and quiet like this, I would almost feel that the river was flowing in me, through my veins, like blood."

Morgan watched him, afraid to breathe. She tried to reconcile what she was hearing with the man she'd met in the Roughneck bar, and couldn't do it.

He bent his head and snorted, then laughed self-consciously. "That must sound really crazy to you, huh?"

"No." The one word escaped her lips like a sigh.

"My father used to bring me here," he went on, picking up a stone and tossing it into the water. It plopped, and ripples fanned out from it, spinning in concentric circles. "He wanted to show me where his family used to live. We would take the canoe down the estuary from the land and sit here, watching the barges, not talking much. He never talked much."

Landry was staring out over the water, not looking at her.

"All his life," Landry said, "my father loved a woman he could never have. I guess that's why he drank, if a drunk needs a reason."

Morgan listened, unsure why he was telling her this.

"He was good to my mother," Landry continued, "as good as he could be within his limitations, but I always sensed there was something wrong there. As I grew I realized that my father had had the one love of his life, and it wasn't my mother."

"Did he ever tell you about her?" Morgan asked. "The woman he loved, I mean?"

Landry shook his head. "He didn't have to. I look like my mother, and I could see him searching my face, wondering why he couldn't see in me the features he wanted to see, the face of the woman who should have been his wife. He drank more and more as he got older, as the one chance he'd had to be happy receded further and further into the past."

"You must have been a comfort to him," Morgan said lamely, unsure how to respond.

Landry shook his head slowly. "Nothing could make up to him for that loss." He flung another stone into the water savagely. "That is not going to happen to me."

Morgan said nothing.

"And my mother, she just...faded. You know how people fade when they aren't cherished, wither like neglected plants?"

"I know," Morgan murmured. "What was she like?"

He shrugged. "Oh, she was one of those resigned types, just took what life handed out to her and didn't complain." He folded his arms on his knees. "She should have fought back more; I think he would have respected her for it."

"Didn't he love her at all?" Morgan asked.

"I know he thought she was a good person, and he tried in his own way, but there's just no substitute for the real thing."

"No, I guess there isn't." Morgan paused, wondering whether to probe what was obviously a painful subject. Curiosity won and she said, "Do you know who she was, the woman he loved?"

He nodded. "She's dead now; they both are. She always used to stop me when she saw me in town and ask how my father was." He smiled bitterly. "She wasn't happy, either."

"Why didn't they get together, Beau?"

"Their families. She had a lot of money; my dad had already lost his. The Landry clan was widely regarded as a bunch of down-at-the-heels eccentrics, living on inflated dreams of past glory. And it didn't help that my father was already something of a hellion, a hard drinker, quick with his fists. Her parents wanted her to marry someone suitable. And she did."

"I see."

He glanced at Morgan directly for the first time since he'd begun his reverie.

"Sorry about the trip down memory lane," he said, gesturing vaguely. "I haven't been here in a long while. I've been up to the main property a lot, getting the restoration under way, but never down here. Seeing it again brought it all back: my father, my mother, their wasted lives."

"Oh, Beau, don't say that. Their lives weren't wasted. They produced you and your sister. Some good came out of all that pain."

He lifted a curl of damp hair from her neck and twirled it around his finger. "And you thought you were in for a nice serene boat ride," he said regretfully. "Instead you get a dunking in the river and an overdose of the Landry family angst."

"I don't mind."

"Some date, huh?"

"It's been very... interesting."

He smiled wryly. "Well, it hasn't been a total loss. At least I got you to take off your clothes." His eyes traveled down her body, scanning the skimpy lace bra and brief panties.

Morgan folded her arms across her breasts.

"Oh, don't cover up," he murmured, leaning in toward her. "You're so beautiful." He tipped her chin up with his forefinger and kissed her lightly, trailing his lips across hers and then pressing harder when she yielded to him, opening her mouth.

Morgan wound her arms around his neck, her fingers tangling in the soft, damp hair at his nape. His skin was still sprinkled with droplets from the river, but warm, radiating body heat. She clung to him as he eased her down onto the grass and lay beside her, cradling her in the crook of one arm.

The sensation of his closeness was overwhelming. He was naked to the waist, and she was wearing almost nothing. She felt enveloped by him, sheltered from the world. His mouth left hers and trailed over her cheek, then her throat, finally seeking the creamy skin of her shoulders. Morgan held his head against her, closing her eyes as he turned his attention to her breasts, tonguing her nipples through the sheer silk net of her bra. The cloth was wet and clammy, and his mouth felt like a furnace burning through it, scorching the sensitive tissue beneath. She moaned softly, pulling him closer.

The sound inflamed him. He lifted his head and kissed her again, wildly, pushing her flat and moving over her. Morgan responded instinctively, pressing against him. The taste and feel of him, the smell of him, were intoxicating. She twined her legs with his, running her hands down the length of his satiny, muscular back. Her nails stung him, and he gasped, lifting her, reaching for the clasp of her bra.

The scrap of lace came away in his hands. Morgan shuddered as he touched her, his work-roughened fingers abrading her smooth flesh. He bent suddenly and buried his face between her breasts, his skin on fire. Morgan arched toward him, lost completely. At that moment she would have done anything he wanted.

When he moved back again she looked up at him, her eyes swimming. He brushed her hair back with a trembling hand and said huskily, "I want to make love to you, right here, now."

Morgan closed her eyes.

"Is that what you want?" he asked.

Morgan bit her lip.

He sat up, drawing her with him. "All right, easy does it," he said soothingly. He folded her into his arms, and she sighed, content for the moment to rest against his shoulder.

"It's going kind of fast, isn't it?" he said quietly.

"Yes."

"Scared?"

"A little."

"I know," he said, caressing her loose hair. She kissed his shoulder luxuriously. He took her by the arms abruptly and set her off from him.

"You'd better not do that," he said flatly. "It's not exactly helping me to stop."

Morgan glanced down, embarrassed. Suddenly conscious of her partial nudity, she crossed her arms over her torso.

"Come on," he said, seeing her reaction. "Let's get back." He stood and took her hand, not looking at her. They ran into the river, and once immersed in the water, Morgan felt better. She swam after him until they reached the boat, and then she realized she didn't know what to do next.

"How do we get back on?" she called to him.

"There's a drop ladder at the back," he replied. She followed, paddling in his wake, and climbed the rope ladder after him. He reached down to help her, then handed her his shirt as she stood, dripping, on the deck.

"Please," he said, giving her the once over and then turning away, "cover up that body before I forget I'm trying to be a gentleman."

Morgan pulled the shirt over her head. His rich masculine fragrance permeated the cloth. The sleeves cascaded over her wrists and the bottom hem draped her thighs.

"That's better," he said dryly. He took a gray sweatshirt from a cupboard and put it on, going into the cabin to start the motor. Morgan waited while he lifted the anchor and got them under way. As soon as they were moving she joined him at the wheel, watching as he guided the craft out into the river.

"You okay, *chère*?" he asked, glancing over his shoulder at her.

"Yes."

"You're not upset, are you?" His dark eyes scanned her face.

"No, not really." Confused was more like it.

"You sure?"

"Yes." Morgan touched the wheel. "May I do that?"

"What?"

"Steer the boat."

"If you like. I'll show you."

The trip back was consumed with a crash course in piloting, and Morgan was glad they could keep their conversation on neutral ground. She was slipping into her clothes prior to getting off the boat when she realized that she had left her bra back at the estuary. Any future visitor there might be in for a surprise.

Landry said little as they got into his car, and Morgan wondered what was going on in his mind. Did this sort of thing happen to him all the time, or was he as shaken as she was? And why hadn't he pressed his advantage back at the river? She'd been caught in the grip of their mutual passion, and he knew it. His retreat, unexpected as it was, made her realize that he was more complex than she had first imagined.

The drive back to the hotel was short. The lobby was still; the tourists had all come in and gone to bed. Landry accompanied Morgan to her room in silence, while she wondered what she was going to say to him when they got there.

The carpeted floor made the hallway seem even quieter than it was. When they were standing outside her door Morgan looked up at him shyly.

"Thank you for showing me the river," she said.

He touched her hair. "You're welcome."

She tried again. "It was very interesting and . . ."

He pulled her into his arms. Morgan sighed and closed her eyes.

"Shh," he murmured. "You don't have to say anything."

They stood for a long moment, just holding each other.

"I know you saw Pete Darriet today," he said suddenly, his mouth moving in her hair.

Morgan stiffened slightly.

"I gave him the time off from work," Landry added.

"I can't discuss what he told me with you," Morgan said.

He held her off and looked into her face. "I know. You just go ahead and do your job. It won't interfere with us."

Morgan didn't reply. She wasn't so sure about that.

He kissed her cheek, then her lips. In seconds he was pressing her to the wall, his body hard against hers.

"Oh, don't," she gasped, tearing her mouth from his. "No more tonight, please."

He let her go instantly. Morgan leaned against the door, fighting the desire to return to him.

"When can I see you again?" he said huskily.

"I don't know."

"I'll call you tomorrow."

"I need time to think, Beau."

He stared at her. "Why? Do you imagine things between us are going to change? When it's this strong, this fast, it doesn't go away."

"How do you know?" Morgan asked. "I suppose this happens to you every day?"

"No," he said evenly. "But I would be foolish if I believed I could 'think' a feeling like this away."

"I just want to consider what I'm doing. Don't call me for a couple of days."

"Are you sorry about what happened tonight?" he asked her, his face going blank.

"I didn't say that."

"Then what? Why this delaying tactic?"

Morgan pressed her palms to her temples. "It's not a tactic. Can't you ever forget that I'm a lawyer for one minute? I'm a woman, too."

"I know you're a woman, Morgan," he said huskily. "No one knows it better than I do."

"Then just trust my feminine instincts," she said. "I'm not saying I won't see you anymore; I just want some breathing room."

"I'll call you in forty-eight hours," he said, relenting. He raised his wrist to look at his watch. "At eleven fifty-five on Sunday night."

Morgan smiled with resignation. "Must you be so literal?"

He shrugged. "You said a couple of days. That's a couple of days." He lifted her chin with his forefinger and compelled her to look into his eyes. "You're not going to change your mind again and decide that you're better off without me?"

"No."

"Promise?"

"I promise."

"Even if the ghost of Learned Hand appears to you in a dream and tells you that I'm going to ruin your concentration on the Sunlite case?"

Morgan laughed. "How do you know about Learned Hand?"

"I roomed with a law student for a while and he was always reading opinions by that guy. What a name, huh? You think his parents knew he was going to grow up to be a judge?"

Morgan put her arms around his waist and kissed his cheek. "Good night, *chèr*."

He grinned, lifting her hair off her neck and bunching it in his fists.

"You imitating me now?" he asked.

"It means 'dear one,' doesn't it?"

"Yes."

"Then I used the right word," Morgan said, releasing him. She stood back and took out her room key.

"What happens if I call you before Sunday night?" he asked, his expression mischievous.

Morgan looked at him.

"Just kidding," he said, holding up his hand. "Sleep tight."

"I'll try." Morgan unlocked the door and slipped inside before her resolve weakened.

She listened until she was sure he had left, then flung herself full length on the bed.

Five

Morgan fell asleep fully dressed and woke the next morning feeling disoriented, her mouth dry and her eyes full of sand. She was stumbling around in her wrinkled clothes when the bellboy arrived with a cable from Julie.

"Arriving 3:00 p.m. today," it read. "Will take cab from airport, at hotel by five. Hold wedding till then."

Ha-ha, Morgan thought sourly, tossing the paper on the bed. Very funny. Well, at least Jerry Sinclair had allowed Julie to come and help her. She wasn't really surprised. Julie could be very persuasive.

Morgan spent the day in her room, tracking down people for interviews. She set up a schedule that would occupy them for the next two weeks. She wanted to be very thorough.

She ordered lunch in her room and got right back on the phone. The afternoon passed quickly and she jumped, startled, when the knock came at her door.

"Let me in," Julie called from the hall. "This suitcase weighs a ton."

Morgan opened the door to find Julie sagging against the wall, her bag at her feet. Her face was the color of Santa's suit.

"Why didn't you tell me about the heat?" she demanded without preliminaries, striding past Morgan and collapsing on the bed. She stretched out blissfully, moaning and kicking off her shoes.

"Welcome to New Orleans," Morgan said, grinning.

"The cab wasn't air-conditioned," Julie gasped. "Can you imagine it? That fool of a cabbie was riding around in it all day without air conditioning."

"He's probably a native," Morgan replied, sitting next to Julie on the bed. "They're used to it."

"How could anybody get used to this weather? It's like hell."

"I imagine hell wouldn't be quite this humid, more of a dry heat, like Arizona."

Julie eyed her narrowly. "Very amusing. Your mood seems to have improved since the last time I talked to you."

"That's gallows humor, don't you recognize it?"

"Case going badly?" Julie asked, standing up and unbuttoning her blouse.

"No. Actually I lined up a number of prospects for us to see in the next couple of weeks. We should get quite a bit of information from them, I think."

"Then it must be Mr. Wrong. What's he been up to?" Julie discarded her blouse and unzipped her skirt.

"He took me on a boat ride up the Mississippi last night," Morgan said.

"Did you see Bret Maverick?" Julie asked, giggling. Her skirt fell to the floor and she reclined again in her teddy. "Those clothes were strangling me."

"I think I'm falling in love with him," Morgan said flatly.

"Bret Maverick?"

"Julie, this is serious."

Julie examined her friend's face. "Yes, I can see that it is," she said thoughtfully.

"I can't believe it's happening to me."

"Why not? You're human, aren't you?"

"I don't want this, not now."

"Looks as if you've got it," Julie sat up. "Do you know what you're doing?"

"No," Morgan said miserably.

"That's what I thought." She sighed. "The entire time we've worked together you've been buried so deep in legal briefs that it would have taken a prospector to find you. Now all of a sudden you're jumping off the deep end and telling me you're in love with a guy you've known for exactly *three days*?"

"You know why I was cautious before," Morgan replied. "I told you all about it."

"You told me the guy you were going with in law school married someone else because her father was going to make him a partner in his law firm."

"That's right. And I wasn't 'going' with him; we were engaged."

"All right, you were engaged. So after that you decided to make your work your life, until your arrival in this benighted burg, whereupon you did a complete turnaround and hooked up, on very short notice I might add, with this . . . oil driller."

"He's not an oil driller. He owns a geophysical surveying company."

"Whatever, he works in the oil fields. And that's not the point, anyway. I know I've been telling you to loosen up and have a good time, but don't you think this is taking my advice to the extreme? You have your first real date in I don't know how long, and now you're in love with the guy?"

"I think I may be, that's all."

"Morgan, it's like emerging from a convent and joining the Rockettes."

"It would help a lot if you didn't lecture me," Morgan said unhappily. "Do you think I wanted this to happen? But it has, and now the question is what am I going to do?"

"Beats me."

Morgan put her chin in her hand. "You know that love potion Isolde gave to Tristan to cast a spell on him?"

Julie blinked. "What are you talking about?"

"Isolde's mother was a witch and she gave her daughter a philter to put in Tristan's wine. It ensured that he could never love another woman but Isolde as long as he lived."

"Oh."

"Do you think Beau got some of that stuff and put it in my drink that night at Antoine's?"

Julie made a face.

"Hey, the headache I had the next morning was pretty bad. And I haven't been able to keep my hands off the guy ever since. Something must account for the way I've taken leave of my senses."

"Oh, so you agree this is rather...uncharacteristic behavior on your part?"

"Of course, Julie, I'm not debating that with you. Why do you think I'm so worried? I've never felt like this before in my life."

"What about your erstwhile fiancé? What was his name—Jim?"

Morgan shook her head. "It wasn't like with Beau, not even close. Jim and I had the same education, we were looking forward to entering the same profession, we had the same goals. It was different."

"Dull, you mean," Julie said, rolling over on the bed. "Sounds dull as dishwater to me. And Mr. Landry is anything but."

"Do you think that's it?"

"Well, I haven't heard you talking about his 'goals.' You don't care what they are, am I right?"

Morgan looked at the floor. "Actually, he told me he wanted to rebuild his ancestral home on the river and restore the family name and..." She paused, then raised her head and shrugged. "You're right. I don't care."

"Do you think we'll have time in the middle of this romantic drama to find out if Sunlite is liable in this case?" Julie asked dryly.

"Don't be sarcastic. It's not becoming."

"Tell that to our fearless leader, Jerry Sinclair. He sends greetings, by the way. And a reminder not to exceed $150 a day."

"This place costs $120 a night! What are we supposed to eat, cat food?"

"Apparently. Never fear, I brought my plastic money. We'll charge at the best restaurants and pay it off later. How was that place you went to with Landry?"

"Antoine's? Expensive, I think. There were no prices on the menu."

"No prices on yours, you mean. His had them."

"How do you know?"

"My sister's boyfriend took us to a place like that once. The bill was shocking."

Julie's sister's boyfriend was famed in song and story, a commodities broker with a bottomless wallet. He had bought Julie's sister a sapphire necklace that somehow wound up in the bathroom drain, but that was another tale for another time.

"I guess Antoine's is out, then," Morgan said. "It's just as well, you can't get in the door anyway."

"You got in."

"Beau has a friend who works there. He took us past the tourists waiting in line."

"You got the royal treatment, then."

"I don't know about that. Beau ordered something inedible for the appetizer. He seemed to think it was very funny when I couldn't get it down."

"Why not?"

"It was on fire. Cajun spices or something. It was like munching a crumbled chili pepper. He, of course, ate his and mine."

"Swine."

"That's what I said. But he made up for it with the rest of the dinner. It was all marvelous."

"Oh, well, with the amount of work you say you've got lined up for us, we'll probably only have time for Chinese take-out anyway. Speaking of work...."

"Do we have to? I'm sick to death of it already."

"Why don't we just go over what you've got so far? I have some catching up to do."

"All right." Morgan went for her briefcase, putting the subject of Beau Landry deliberately out of her mind.

Landry reached for the phone, then withdrew his hand. He had a date, which he wanted to break, but he wasn't quite callous enough to do it. He didn't want to think of himself as the type who'd break a date at the last minute because he'd met another woman he liked better.

He stood to change his clothes and face the inevitable. Judy Belleau was a nice girl, but after the past few days with Morgan he could barely remember what she looked like. He had a vague impression of dark eyes and even teeth combined with a chatty personality. She wore odd clothes, he recalled—outré glossy-magazine-type things with big chunky metal jewelry, heavy links about the neck that made her look as if she'd just escaped from a chain gang and called to mind Marley's ghost. And her hair was too short, cut like a boy's. It made her ears stick out, weighted down by the unidentified clinking objects hanging from them. He couldn't imagine why he'd asked her out; whatever appeal she'd once had faded in the glow of Morgan's memory like a distant star eclipsed by the sun.

As he dressed, Landry paced around his condominium. It overlooked the river and had cost too much when he'd bought it a year earlier. He'd purchased the thing in the first place because renting was costing him a fortune in taxes; he needed the owner's deduction to offset his growing income. But it had never seemed like home to him, especially after the decorator had transformed it into a "bachelor pad": chrome and glass and stark Swedish modern furniture. It looked and felt like a hospital.

Belle Isle was home. He couldn't wait until the house was finished and he could move there. In retrospect he realized that dragging Morgan out to the river was probably a childish and impulsive idea, but the sentiment that had impelled him to do it remained. He'd felt such a

FREE BOOKS!

FREE GIFTS!

PLAY THE "LUCKY 7" SLOT MACHINE GAME!

AND YOU COULD GET FREE BOOKS, AND SURPRISE GIFTS!

NO COST! NO OBLIGATION!
NO PURCHASE NECESSARY!

PLAY ''LUCKY 7''
AND GET AS MANY AS SIX FREE GIFTS . . .

HOW TO PLAY:

1. With a coin, carefully scratch off the three silver boxes at the right. This makes you eligible to receive one or more free books, and possibly other gifts, depending on what is revealed beneath the scratch-off area.

2. You'll receive brand-new Silhouette Desire® novels, never before published. When you return this card, we'll send you the books and gifts you qualify for *absolutely free*!

3. And, a month later, we'll send you 6 additional novels to read and enjoy. If you decide to keep them, you'll pay only $2.24 per book, a savings of 26¢ per book. There are no hidden extras.

4. We'll also send you additional free gifts from time to time, as well as our newsletter.

5. You must be completely satisfied, or you may return a shipment of books and cancel at any time.

This may be your lucky play...
FREE BOOKS and FREE GIFTS???
Scratch off the three silver boxes
and mail us your card today!

PLAY "LUCKY 7"

Just scratch off the three silver boxes with a coin.
Then check below to see which gifts you get.

YES! I have scratched off the silver boxes. Please send me
all the gifts for which I qualify. I understand I am under no
obligation to purchase any books, as explained on the opposite
page.   225 CIL JAYN

_____

NAME

_____

ADDRESS   APT

_____

CITY   STATE   ZIP

7	7	7	WORTH FOUR FREE BOOKS, FREE SURPRISE GIFT AND MYSTERY BONUS
🍒	🍒	🍒	WORTH FOUR FREE BOOKS AND FREE SURPRISE GIFT
●	●	●	WORTH FOUR FREE BOOKS
🔔	🔔	🍒	WORTH TWO FREE BOOKS

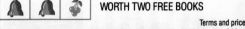

DETACH AND MAIL CARD TODAY

BUSINESS REPLY CARD

First Class   Permit No. 717   Buffalo, NY

Postage will be paid by addressee

SILHOUETTE BOOKS®
901 Fuhrmann Blvd.,
P.O. Box 1867
Buffalo, NY 14240-9952

NO POSTAGE
NECESSARY
IF MAILED
IN THE
UNITED STATES

strong connection with her, almost from the first, that having her see and understand his obsession had quickly become an obsession in itself. His disappointment when she quite sensibly resisted his plan to travel up the estuary had been acute. In his mind he had merely postponed the trip until a later time, when he would take her by daylight. And by the road.

He surveyed himself in the mirrored door of his closet. The whole apartment was a monument to vanity, with mirrors in every conceivable spot. Catching sight of himself so often still made him nervous. He adjusted the collar of his shirt, wondering what Morgan was doing. He hoped that she was closeted with a stack of paperwork; he couldn't bear the thought that she might be out socially, perhaps meeting someone else. He glanced at his watch. Only twenty-eight hours to go before he could call her.

It seemed like an eternity; he felt the longing for her presence like a physical pain. He was still amazed that he'd been able to stop when he was making love to her on the riverbank. Under ordinary circumstances he would have carried those preliminaries to their conclusion, but the circumstances with Morgan were not ordinary. She had looked up at him with those drowned eyes, obviously scared but equally obviously lost, and for the first time in his life compassion had outrun desire. He had let her go, and he was not sorry.

His problem now was guilt, and guilt was a cancer. He couldn't rid himself of the image of Morgan, listening diligently, faithfully recording his answers to her questions, planning her strategy for the Sunlite case based on what he said. He kept telling himself that he'd done what he had to do, but that didn't make him feel any better.

Why did he have to meet her this way? It wasn't fair. He'd been lonely as only a man who'd been through a long string of casual affairs could be lonely. He'd always thought he didn't have time for a special woman because he was so busy with his work, but that wasn't the reason. He hadn't met the right woman. You made time for the right one, he discovered. Work became less important, everything became less important. It was happening to him right now.

But before he could do anything about it, he had to take Judy Belleau to a Sibelius concert. Whoever Sibelius was. He'd told her to choose where she would like to go, and that was her answer. He'd dutifully bought the tickets and, judging by the crowd waiting in line, he was going to fit in like reindeer at an Easter parade.

Landry picked up his car keys from his dresser and left.

"Let's go and take a walk," Julie said.

"Aren't you tired from the trip?" Morgan asked.

"I could use the fresh air. I'm going cross-eyed from looking at these papers." She shoved a stack onto the floor and stood up, going to get her suitcase.

"I thought it was too hot out for you," Morgan reminded her.

"It's ten o'clock. It should have cooled off by now. And I'm absolutely starving. Don't you ever think about food?"

"There's room service," Morgan said.

"I have cabin fever, too. Don't be so argumentative. Come on, humor me." She pulled a tank top and a cotton skirt from her case and slipped into them, fluffing her reddish hair with her fingers.

"Oh, all right," Morgan said. She glanced in the mirror, decided that she would do, and shouldered her purse.

"What's open around here at night?" Julie asked as they went into the hall.

"Everything, apparently. It's tourist season. There's a seafood place called Arnaud's a few blocks away that's supposed to be very nice."

"Sounds good."

They descended in the elevator and took a leisurely walk to the restaurant. It had indeed cooled off, and the streets were full of pedestrians enjoying the break from the heat. They had a late dinner and were strolling out through Arnaud's Victorian doors to the sidewalk when Morgan almost crashed into Beau Landry—and the woman accompanying him.

All four participants in the scene stared at one another, as if caught in the wrong bed in the second act of a French farce. Morgan and Landry looked stricken, Julie looked expectant, and Judy Belleau looked bewildered—she didn't know who anybody was.

Silence reigned for an endless moment. Landry was the first to recover. He cleared his throat and said calmly, "Hello, Morgan."

"Hello, Beau," Morgan murmured.

"I'd like you to meet Judy Belleau," he went on. "Judy, this is Morgan Taylor."

The two women nodded. "My friend, Julie Bannister," Morgan said, indicating Julie. "Beau Landry."

More nods. "Pleased to meet you," Landry said.

"How do you do," Julie said, her eyes fixed on Landry's face.

"What are you doing here?" Landry asked Morgan.

"We just had a late dinner inside," she replied, trying not to gape at Judy, who was wearing a week of Morgan's salary on her back.

"Isn't it a cute place?" Judy said. "We were just going in to have a drink at the bar. We've been to a concert and the air conditioning wasn't working right in the hall. It was so hot that we're both parched."

"Don't let us keep you," Morgan said, moving past them.

Landry put his hand on her arm. "I'll call you," he said meaningfully.

"Good night," Morgan replied, looking at Julie, who was rooted to the spot.

"It was nice meeting you," Julie said.

"Same here," Landry replied automatically.

Julie didn't move.

Morgan was just about to kick her when Julie galvanized herself into action and followed Morgan through the door.

"Will you wait a minute?" she demanded, glancing back over her shoulder.

"Not here," Morgan replied through clenched teeth. She kept up a brisk pace, Julie trotting alongside her, until they had put some distance between themselves and the restaurant.

"Morgan," Julie said, more insistently, and Morgan stopped, turning to look at her.

"He was on a date with that woman," Julie said.

"Oh, thank you, Julie, for making that clear," Morgan said.

"She was very chic."

"Thanks again, pal."

"Well, she was. Did you see those clothes? And that hair? She made me feel like Mammy Yokum."

"You're cheering me up immensely," Morgan responded, starting to walk again.

Julie trailed behind her, saying, "I don't know if I agreed with those earrings, though. I think they would have gone better on a Somali tribeswoman."

"I can't believe my rotten luck," Morgan ranted, not listening. "Do you know how many people live in New Orleans? Do you know how many people are *visiting* at this very moment? Do you know the odds against my running into him that way?"

"Who do I look like, Mr. Spock?" Julie replied.

"God, I feel like such a fool," Morgan said. "He materialized like an apparition right in front of me. I was speechless."

"I wish he would materialize in front of me," Julie said fervently. "I wouldn't be tongue-tied, that much I can tell you."

"He took her to a concert," Morgan said unnecessarily.

"I felt compelled to point out that he was not killing time figuring crossword puzzles until he saw you again," Julie stated.

"You're doing wonders for my ego this evening," Morgan said. "I'm so glad you came down here to help me."

"It's the truth."

"I know it's the truth, but I have no right to complain. I've known him only a few days, and we haven't made any commitments to each other."

"I think you've made a commitment," Julie said quietly. "In your heart."

"He's free to date anyone he wants," Morgan said, ignoring that.

"Right."

"He probably knew her a long time before he met me."

"I agree."

"We only went out twice, and once was business."

"Uh-huh."

Morgan turned to Julie at the hotel entrance. "Then why do I feel so wretched?" she asked hopelessly.

"Because you're already hung up on the guy," Julie replied. "And tonight was an indication that he doesn't feel the same way."

Morgan nodded wearily. "Oh, let's go inside," she said. "I've had enough of this night. I just want to get to bed and forget it."

But she discovered that it wasn't so easy to forget it. Morgan lay awake for a long time, hours after Julie was breathing evenly in sleep, replaying the scene in her mind.

He had gone from their embraces on the riverbank to a date with another woman. She had imagined him sitting at home, waiting for the time to pass until he could call her again, and instead he was out on the town with that sophisticated lady enjoying some music and having a late drink.

Learn from this, she told herself sternly. Don't be taken in by the stories about the old homestead and his considerable charm. Grow up, don't be fooled, be mature.

But she still felt like crying. She was staring dry-eyed at the ceiling tiles, visible by the light from the adjoining bathroom, when the telephone rang.

She jumped and glanced at the bedside clock. It was one-fifteen in the morning.

She picked up the receiver. Julie rolled over, grumbling in her sleep.

"Hello?" Morgan said.

"Miss Taylor, this is the night desk clerk. I'm sorry to disturb you at this late hour, but there's a gentleman here who insists on speaking to you. He says it's an emergency.''

"What's his name?" Morgan said, as if she didn't know.

"It's a Mr. Landry." Morgan could hear Beau's voice in the background saying, "Just give me the phone."

"I'll speak to him," Morgan said. There was a rustling sound and then Beau said, "Morgan, we have to talk."

"Beau, do you know what time it is?"

"I don't care what time it is. I want to talk to you right now."

"It's the middle of the night!"

"So what? You weren't sleeping. Are you going to see me, or what?"

"Beau, Julie is asleep and . . ."

"And who the hell is Julie?" he demanded, annoyed. "You told me you were working on this case alone, and all of a sudden, out of nowhere, she turns up?"

"We decided there was more work involved than we thought at first, and she came down to help me."

"Chaperon you," he corrected. "Well, she's too late."

"Beau, can't this wait?" Morgan said impatiently.

"No. I want to explain about Judy."

"You don't owe me any explanation," Morgan replied stiffly.

"It's not a question of owing anything. I want you to understand why I was with her. Come downstairs and meet me in the all-night coffee shop off the lobby."

"Beau, this is ridiculous."

"Do you want me to come up there?" he threatened.

Julie sat up in bed, her bangs in parentheses on her forehead, her face swollen with sleep. "Wassa madder?" she mumbled.

"I'll meet you," Morgan whispered savagely into the phone. "Just give me time to change."

"I'll be waiting," he answered, and the line went dead.

"Whose onna phone?" Julie queried.

"It's nothing, go back to sleep. I'll handle it."

Julie crumpled bonelessly back onto her pillow. In seconds she was breathing deeply again.

Morgan shot out of bed, pulling off her nightgown, muttering to herself. She dressed in the dark, putting on the same clothes she had taken off earlier, feeling grubby. She felt her way into the bathroom and shut the door before turning on the overhead light.

The woman in the mirror looked as though she had been lying in bed for two hours on the verge of tears. Morgan splashed her face vigorously with cold water and ran a brush through her hair. She patted powder on her nose and rubbed lip gloss on her mouth. Then she tiptoed past Julie, grabbed her room key, and ran down the stairs.

Landry was waiting for her in a booth near the entrance to the coffee shop. He jumped up and came to her side as she walked through the door. Except for the cashier, they were the only two people in the place.

"I'm glad you came," he said to her. He was still wearing the same clothes he'd had on when they'd met in the street earlier that night.

"I didn't have much choice," Morgan replied coolly. "I don't think Julie would have been able to take one of your theatrical arrivals."

"You're mad at me," he said flatly.

"Why should I be mad at you? You promised that you wouldn't call me for two days, and instead you break that promise by ringing my hotel room in the wee hours of the morning."

"I made that promise under duress and, besides, you know why I had to call."

"Do I?"

"You were upset when you saw me with Judy, and that's the real reason you're angry with me now."

"Don't flatter yourself."

He sighed. "Let's sit down, okay?" He led her to the booth he had occupied alone and they sat facing one another.

"Morgan, listen to me," he began.

"I'm listening," she answered crisply.

"I made that date with Judy before I met you and, believe me, I gave serious consideration to breaking it."

"Your social life is none of my business," Morgan said flatly, staring over his shoulder.

"Look at me," he commanded.

Morgan did so.

"It is your business now," he said quietly. "I know that, even if you don't."

Morgan said nothing.

"I just thought that calling Judy up at the last minute and telling her I couldn't go was a lousy thing to do. She was looking forward to that concert and it didn't seem right."

Morgan couldn't argue with him.

"I won't see her again," he added.

"You don't have to say that," Morgan told him.

"I want to." He held her gaze until she looked away.

There was a long pause.

"So how was the concert?" she asked brightly, looking back at him.

He shook his head. "I don't know. It didn't make much of an impression. I spent the whole time thinking about you. And then after I saw you outside that restaurant I really felt like a jerk. The minute I dropped Judy off at her house I came straight here. She lives quite a distance away or I would have made it earlier.''

The cashier, who was apparently doubling as waitress, appeared at their table.

"Two coffees," Landry said shortly, and she went away again.

"Got rid of her," he muttered, and Morgan smiled.

"Ah, a smile," he said in a wondering tone. "I thought you had forgotten how to smile."

"No, I'm just tired," Morgan said.

"And hurt, and disappointed," he finished for her.

"Yes," Morgan admitted, her voice barely audible.

He reached across the table and took her hand in his. Her slim fingers were swallowed up in his callused, work-roughened palm.

"I know how you felt on the river," he said quietly. "I felt the same. And I know that if I had seen you out with another man so soon after that it would have been like a knife in my gut."

The waitress arrived with two cups of coffee and wordlessly plunked them down in front of each of them, spilling the liquid into the saucers as she did so. She added a tin pitcher of cream and a glass bowl of sugar and stalked off.

"She's a charmer, isn't she?" Landry asked, releasing Morgan's hand.

"What do you want? It's 2:00 a.m."

He took a sip of his drink and grimaced. "Tastes like a truck tire was boiled in it."

"Well, we didn't come here for the cuisine," Morgan pointed out to him. She left her cup untouched.

"Am I forgiven?" he said softly.

"There's nothing to forgive; you did the right thing. Of course you couldn't lie to that girl, and telling her the truth would have been worse."

He took her hand and held it to his lips. "Morgan, this is driving me crazy. Can't we go upstairs to your room and . . ."

"Julie is in my room."

"Can't we get her another room?"

"My firm won't pay for it."

"I'll pay for it. Put her in the bridal suite for all I care. I want some privacy."

"Beau, I can't let you do that."

He looked at the ceiling, then back at her. "Well, what about tomorrow, then?"

"Beau, tomorrow is Sunday and the people we need to talk to about this case are off work. I have to spend the day interviewing some of them. It's the only free time they have."

"Tomorrow night, then."

"All right."

"Are you sure? You're not going to decide you need to interview the president or something?"

She just looked at him.

"Okay, let's blow this joint." He stood and she did, also, waiting as he left some money on the table. They walked out together.

"I'll take you up to your room," he said.

"No, Beau, it's better that we say goodbye here," Morgan replied as they approached the elevator.

"You don't want me to scandalize Julie by making passionate love to you outside the door?" he asked.

Morgan smiled. "Something like that. Although she would probably sleep through it."

"You wouldn't," he said, and she could feel her face growing warm.

"Good night, Beau."

He kissed her mouth lightly. "Good night, *chère*. I'll call you around six, okay?"

"Okay."

She stepped into the elevator and he walked away.

Six

Sunday passed quickly. Morgan and Julie interviewed witnesses all day long, and by late afternoon Julie was ready for a diversion. She settled for teasing Morgan.

"I thought I heard some heavy breathing outside the door last night," she observed, clipping together a series of pages and sliding them into a folder.

"You were dead to the world," Morgan replied tartly. "You wouldn't have responded to an air raid siren."

"I heard the phone when it rang," she said stoutly. Then she looked puzzled. "Or I dreamed of it ringing." She labeled the folder and put it aside.

"You heard it, mumbled something, and returned immediately to sleep." Morgan slipped the cassette of her last interview into an envelope and sealed it. Some people objected to being taped, but she occasionally found it useful to record those who didn't mind it.

"So tell me what Landry said," Julie demanded.

"I already told you."

"No, you didn't. You told me he explained that he'd made the date with that girl before he met you and didn't want to break it."

"That's what he said."

"Details! I want details!" Julie insisted. "It must have been more interesting than you're making it sound. He called you at what time? Sounds like he was pretty impatient to clear up any misunderstanding."

"I suppose so," Morgan admitted.

"'I suppose so,'" Julie imitated her. "Aren't we cool and collected? I seem to recall you were pretty upset last night."

Morgan threw her a look.

"Don't make faces at me, Morgan. If that guy were chasing me all over New Orleans I wouldn't be pretending a serenity I didn't feel."

"He's not chasing me all over New Orleans."

"What do you call it?"

"He's . . . well . . . he's interested."

"Interested enough to turn green when you caught him out with somebody else after knowing him only a few days. Did you see the look on his face when you came through that door?"

"I imagine I didn't look much better," Morgan said dryly.

"Who was his date, anyway?" Julie asked curiously.

"Julie, I don't know. I didn't interrogate him about it. I just listened to what he had to say."

"She looked very . . . groomed," Julie said diplomatically.

"I saw her, too, remember?" Morgan replied. "No need to restrain yourself. She looked like she had stepped straight from the pages of a fashion magazine."

"Well," Julie observed kindly, "some men aren't really impressed by those model-y types."

"Let's hope Beau's one of them, or he won't be hanging out with yours truly for too long," Morgan said lightly.

"You're thin enough to be a model," Julie said loyally.

"Thank you, but we both know how I would look in those exotic duds."

"Like you were dressed up in your mother's clothes?" Julie suggested.

"Exactly. It has to be toned down and conservative or else I resemble Minnie Mouse outfitted for Mickey's birthday."

"It isn't that bad," Julie said, giggling.

"It certainly is. Remember the time you went shopping with me? Remember how I looked in that fur-trimmed jacket?"

Julie's giggles escalated into laughter. "The salesgirl couldn't believe it. It looked great on the hanger."

"But not on me."

"You looked like you were wearing one of those ice-skating outfits, like Sonja Henie in the movies."

"Thank you," Morgan responded, pretending to be offended.

"And that plaid suit," Julie went on, remembering. "It looked like a private school uniform."

"I think that's sufficient discussion," Morgan said crisply. "My ego is fragile enough."

The telephone rang.

"Hark!" Julie said in a stage whisper, putting her hand over her heart.

"Oh, shut up," Morgan muttered, going to the bedside stand and lifting the receiver. "Hello," she said in as cultured a tone as she could muster.

"Hi, *chère*," Landry said.

"Six o'clock," Morgan said to him, glancing at her travel alarm.

"You could set your watch by me," he confirmed. "So what are we doing tonight?"

"Anything you like," Morgan answered.

"Anything?"

"Within reason," she amended quickly.

"Aw, shucks," he said, laughing. "What if I were to suggest something unreasonable? Oh, wait, I did that already, didn't I? No canoes for you, right?"

"Beau, I didn't mean that I wouldn't go to Belle Isle with you. Just not that way."

"Okay. We'll go the civilized route, by car: wheels, a roof, steering wheel, everything."

"I'm relieved to hear it."

"But for tonight, how about some jazz? I know a great little club in the Garden District; the sax player is fabulous."

"You must really like music. You were at a concert last night, too."

"Well, I wouldn't really call that music. It was more like a long nap with some instruments snoozing along in the background."

"Oh, I see. You like your music a little hotter, I take it."

"That's right. And for Le Jazz Hot, Rudy's is the place. Seven okay?"

"Seven is fine. I'll meet you downstairs in the lobby."

"You'll know me. I'll be the guy with the canoe."

"Enough already with the canoe jokes, buddy."

His earthy chuckle came over the wire.

"See you in a few minutes, *chère*," he said, and then the line went dead.

"Not wasting any time, is he?" Julie greeted Morgan as she turned from the phone. "You barely have time to get changed."

"You listened to the entire conversation?"

"Well, I was right here. What was I supposed to do, lock myself in the bathroom?" Julie said indignantly.

"So how will you occupy yourself while I'm gone?" Morgan asked, unbuttoning her blouse.

"Oh, don't worry about me," Julie said airily, "I'll just sit here and . . . knit."

"Watch television."

"The hotel portable features snow on five of the seven stations."

"Read."

"You know I can't read anything but legal briefs," Julie admonished.

"Excuse me for suggesting it. Do your nails."

"The only shade of polish I brought with me is called 'Tangerine Temptation,' and I'm fairly sure that the way things are going I will not be able to live up to the name."

"You're whining, Julie." Morgan tossed her blouse on a chair and went to the closet.

"Easy for you to say. You're heading out on the town with that divine man, and I'm going to be sitting here with the summer reruns. *You* should use the nail polish."

"Why don't you get your hair done? The salon downstairs is open every evening until nine."

Julie brightened. "I could use a new do. Maybe that's a good idea."

Morgan slipped into a sleeveless shell and patted her friend's shoulder as she passed. "Have you seen my beige skirt?" she asked.

"Hanging on the back of the bathroom door," Julie answered. "Which one of us is going to call Joking Jerry Sinclair tomorrow?"

"Oh, do we have to?" Morgan asked, dismayed.

"I promised him a report every couple of days. A condition of my release."

"I'll call him, then," Morgan sighed as she zipped her skirt. "It's supposed to be my case."

"Tell him you're on the verge of a breakthrough. That's the kind of thing he likes to hear."

"Julie, you're a shameless liar. You know this case looks bad for Sunlite."

"I suggest you don't give him that unwelcome news right now."

Morgan began brushing her hair. "All the people I talked to were very down on Sunlite. The company was running a shoddy operation."

Julie nodded. "No one was surprised by the accident."

"We're going to be mighty unpopular at TA for coming to this conclusion," Morgan observed. "We're talking megabucks here."

Julie shrugged. "They can afford it."

Morgan put down her brush and picked up her lipstick. "Do you think this top is all right?" she asked, examining herself critically in the mirror.

"I don't think that guy would notice if you were wearing sackcloth," Julie answered. "I know an infatuated male when I see one."

"Well, I'm off," Morgan announced, picking up her purse. "I feel a little guilty going out and leaving you here alone."

"You should."

"Are you sure you'll be all right?"

"Morgan, what's the matter with you? I'm just kidding. Go and have a wonderful time. I'm not five. I'll get my hair done and relax for the evening. Goodbye."

"Goodbye." Morgan left the room to go down to the lobby.

Landry was waiting for her. He stepped forward as the elevator doors opened to reveal her.

"Hi," he said. He was wearing a pale green shirt in handkerchief cotton with light gray summer slacks.

"Hi, Beau."

He reached for her hand and she slipped it into his.

"I didn't really ask you if you liked jazz," he said as they walked to the main door. "Do you?"

Morgan shrugged. "I haven't had much exposure to it, just Ella Fitzgerald records. But I'm curious."

"It sounds like noise to some people."

"Noise?"

"Yeah, you know, discord. Sometimes if you don't grow up with it you don't understand it."

"Don't worry, I'm open-minded. When it comes to entertainment, anyway."

During the ride to the club Landry gave Morgan a short history of jazz, discussing the greats—names she had never heard of—and the development of the music through the years. It was obviously a hobby, even a passion, of his, and she enjoyed listening to him. His enthusiasm was catching.

The club was down a flight of slate steps from the street, set behind one of the grilled gates that were everywhere in the district. The music drifted out into the street, and when Landry opened the door it flowed over them.

The club was tiny, and it was jammed. The air was thick, blue with smoke, and Morgan could barely see where they were going. Landry corralled somebody who led them to a table in a corner near the band. Morgan sank into her seat gratefully, noticing that most of the patrons were standing.

A soloist commanded the piano, and the rest of the musicians backed her up with a wailing saxophone and an assortment of other instruments. Landry ordered something to drink and then leaned across the table to Morgan.

"What do you think?" he asked, raising his voice to be heard above the music.

"It's very...atmospheric," she said, unable to describe the overwhelming ambiance of the place any better. Suddenly the music ceased and the piano player adjusted a microphone perched on a music stand.

"Solo coming up," Landry said to Morgan during the lull. "She's really fine. You're in for a treat."

The woman, an attractive black with salt-and-pepper hair, began tinkling along the keys while the other musicians took a rest.

"Is that 'Bill Bailey'?" Morgan asked, listening.

Landry nodded.

"That's one of the few jazz songs I'd recognize," Morgan said, and he grinned.

The woman began to sing, softly at first, then with increasing fervor. After the first verse she repeated the chorus, and many of the onlookers sang along.

"That rainy evening, you threw me out, with nothing but a fine tooth comb," Morgan sang, then stopped self-consciously when she saw that Landry was watching her with a half smile on his face.

"What?" she said.

"You memorized the words?" he asked.

"My father used to sing it."

"Was he a jazz fan?"

"Not really, but he liked this one."

"Everybody does."

The soloist finished her bit, and the band took over for a Dixieland number that started Morgan's foot tapping.

"Do you like it?" Landry asked, almost shouting.

Morgan nodded vigorously, not trusting her voice.

Their drinks came. Landry bolted his shot, and Morgan took a sip of her drink, discovering that it was soda. He must have noticed her lack of interest in the wine at Antoine's.

"Okay?" he said, gesturing toward her glass.

She nodded again.

Dixieland gave way to another number, and then a break. Morgan's ears were ringing.

"Would you like to go outside for some air?" Landry asked her, and she smiled.

"Thanks, I would."

He took her hand and led her to the back of the club, where a door opened onto an alley. They ascended stone steps and Morgan found herself in a small, walled garden.

"This isn't for the patrons, is it?" she asked nervously, looking around. It appeared to be private property.

"It's all right, don't worry."

"Do you know the owner?" she asked suspiciously.

He grinned mysteriously.

"Let me rephrase that. Do you know everybody in New Orleans?"

He laughed. "Not yet. But I'm working on it."

The oleander and hibiscus were in bloom, and their fragrance scented the air, the blossoms a vivid counterpoint to the summer dusk. The cooling trend had continued, and a light pleasant breeze caressed Morgan's cheek and ruffled Landry's dark hair.

"It's a beautiful night," she said softly.

"And you're a beautiful lady," he replied, touching her mouth with his forefinger.

"Let lips do what hands do," Morgan whispered, and he kissed her.

The kiss didn't stop when the music began again inside. When he finally released her, he said huskily, "Do you want to go back in there?"

Morgan shook her head mutely.

"Will you come home with me?" he asked, his voice low, uncertain.

Morgan's heart was pounding, but she made a decision to take a chance. If she loved him, she loved him.

"Let's go," she said, and he took her arm.

Seven

The trip to Landry's apartment was conducted in silence. Morgan was so nervous that her hands were clammy despite the car's air conditioning, and she hardly noticed as he turned the car into the parking lot of a modern high-rise building overlooking the river. When he shut off the ignition the sudden silence amplified the sound of their breathing in the confined space.

Morgan turned to look at him. He was watching her intently.

"Changed your mind?" he said softly.

Morgan shook her head.

"That wasn't very convincing," he commented dryly. He draped his arm along the back of her seat and slid his fingers under her hair, gripping the nape of her neck. Morgan reacted to his touch, sighing and dropping her eyes.

"Look at me," he said.

She raised them again.

"I'll take you home if you say so," he told her gently, caressing her skin. "I will not lead you into something you don't want."

"I want, Beau," Morgan whispered. "I want you more than any man I ever met."

He closed his eyes, dark lashes sweeping his cheeks, and his hand slipped from her neck.

"Don't say that to me," he muttered. "We may never get out of this car." He folded his hands, as if to occupy them, and waited. It was clear that the next move would be hers.

Morgan swallowed hard. "This is where you live?" she said stupidly.

He smiled. "That's why we're here."

"The building's very nice," Morgan commented.

"Yes."

"New. Very modern," she added, wondering when she would exhaust her supply of inane pleasantries.

He nodded.

"I think I'd like to see the inside," Morgan said bravely, and he squeezed her shoulder briefly before he got out to open her door.

They walked together across the parking lot and up a flagstone path to the main entrance, double oak doors with glass cameo insets, fitted with brass. The lobby was paved with Mexican tiles and overflowing with plants. It was monitored by a uniformed doorman with a computerized security system.

"Mr. Landry," the doorman said, nodding.

"Hey, Joe," Landry replied, shepherding Morgan past the man and punching the button for the elevator. Morgan wondered how many other female visitors had witnessed Joe's discreet greeting, and then shoved the thought out of her mind. Tonight she would live for the moment and let the future take care of itself.

The elevator was equipped with Muzak, and Landry crossed his eyes as the speaker segued from "Strangers in the Night" to "The Summer Wind."

"I've been meaning to speak to them about including some Muddy Waters in their repertoire," he said lightly.

Morgan laughed, trying to feign a casual attitude.

The elevator opened onto a carpeted hallway. The entrances to duplicate apartments faced each other. It was obvious that together the two suites took up the whole floor.

"Left," Landry said, and Morgan turned, following him to the black enameled door he indicated. He unlocked it and they stepped into a mirrored foyer with a black-and-white diamond pattern on the floor and a cutglass fixture overhead. It blazed with light when Landry flicked a switch on the wall.

"Go on in," he said to Morgan, stopping to press a series of numbers on an alarm panel. She walked ahead into a large living room, which was flanked by a kitchen with a breakfast nook on the left and bedrooms on the right. Sheer drapes ran from floor to ceiling along two walls, concealing a balcony overlooking the river. Glass tables sat on a gray-and-black Oriental rug. A gray plush sofa was complemented by black leather occasional chairs on either side of a stone fireplace. Brass lamps with silk shades matched the brass frames on the wall hangings.

The whole apartment was as immaculate as an operating room.

"Feel like you're checking into a clinic?" Landry asked at her shoulder.

His question so accurately reflected what she was thinking that she suppressed a grin.

"When the decorator was finished I wound up with the waiting room of a dentist's office," he said, tossing his keys on the coffee table. "Every time I come home I expect to get my teeth drilled."

"It's really very nice, it just needs to be...personalized a little more," Morgan said.

"Yeah, well, I'm not here much. I guess it shows." He walked to a well-stocked liquor cabinet against the wall and asked, "Would you like a drink?"

When Morgan hesitated, he said, "Oh, I forgot what a booze hound you are. There's some soda in the fridge." He splashed amber liquid into a glass for himself. "Cola or something else?"

"Cola's fine."

He got her a soft drink from the kitchen and then pulled the drapes back from the windows with a single movement. They whispered along a ceiling track and folded into corners, revealing the river shimmering below them. Landry unlatched the glass doors and they stepped out onto the balcony.

"This is lovely," Morgan said softly, taking in the boats traveling at a leisurely pace on the water, the glittering lights on the opposite bank.

He nodded, sipping his scotch and then setting his glass on the rail. "The view sold me on the place. And even on the hottest night you can catch a breeze out here."

"Yes, I can feel it," Morgan said.

She gazed out over the water until she sensed him staring at her.

"What is it?" she asked.

He looked away, then laughed self-consciously. "Well, having achieved my heart's desire in getting you here, I don't seem to know what to do next."

Morgan put her glass down next to his and turned to face him.

"Was it really your heart's desire to get me here?" she asked quietly, reaching up to touch his face.

He closed his eyes, then nodded.

"Oh, Beau," she whispered, and put her head on his shoulder. He smoothed her hair for a moment, as if assuring himself of her presence, before pulling her into his arms.

Morgan savored the sensation of his closeness, drinking in his unique scent, a combination of starch from his shirt, the clean shampoo fragrance of his hair and the blood heat of his dusky skin. His body exuded a sense of strength and solidity as pervasive as the aura of masculinity that surrounded him. She knew she was powerless, and submitted, turning her face up for his kiss when she felt him stir against her.

His mouth tasted faintly of liquor, but more of him, his full underlip cushioning hers as his large hands spanned her waist. He straddled her, pressing her back into the railing, his mouth moving to her cheek and then her neck as she gripped him for support. They remained lost in each other until the horn of a passing boat startled them, and they sprang apart.

Morgan looked down to see a group of tourists on the bow of a pleasure cruiser waving up at them. Wolf whistles carried across the water with surprising clarity.

"Oh, no," Morgan moaned, burying her face against Landry's chest. He was laughing.

"Riverside entertainment, free of charge," he said. "They're getting their money's worth."

"How embarrassing," Morgan muttered.

"Let's go inside," Landry said. "They've seen enough."

He led her through the glass doors and locked them, pulling the drapes closed. He turned to find Morgan standing uncertainly behind him.

"Have a seat," he said casually, and she sat gingerly on the velvety sofa, smoothing her skirt over her knees.

"Get comfortable, kick off your shoes."

She obeyed.

He sat near her in one of the leather chairs, slouching and extending his legs, and said brightly, "So, how about those Phillies?"

Morgan giggled, her nervousness dissipating.

"Not a baseball fan?" he said. "Hockey's always good. Like the Flyers?"

She made a face at him.

"Speak up," he cautioned her. "I'm running out of topics. Next comes inflation, the common market and, last but not least, that old standard, the weather."

"Beau."

"Yes?" His dark brows shot up in a parody of inquiry.

"What does a geophysical surveyor do?"

He groaned. "Not my job. That's boring."

"Not to me. I don't know anything about it."

He shrugged. "Well, up until recently my main business was locating underground reservoirs and sinking oil wells. But, as you may know, the oil business hasn't been so hot lately, and so I've expanded into other areas—land surveying for developers, tapping ground water for private wells, putting in sand-mound cisterns and septic tanks. I can do almost anything that requires figuring out the subsurface and using it to advantage. I'm a lot better off than the drillers and roughnecks who depended on the oil boom for survival. A lot of them are out of work.''

"So you adapted," Morgan said thoughtfully.

"Survival of the fittest," he replied. "Nature's law. I'm a classic example of Darwinian evolution."

"That would mean that the Sunlite project was just about the last oil job you worked on," she commented.

"That's right, but we're not going to talk about that tonight," he warned. "The word 'Sunlite' is excised from your vocabulary as of this moment."

"Oh, all right," Morgan agreed. "But that case is the reason we met."

"That doesn't mean we have to spend every waking moment beating it to death." He got up and moved next to her, taking her hand. "There are more interesting things to discuss."

"Such as."

"Well, your skin, for one. The back of your hand, for example. Do you see how the surface is so smooth and creamy, and these little freckles are so tempting? It looks like an eggnog sprinkled with nutmeg."

"Beau, that is the most ridiculous thing I've ever heard," Morgan replied, laughing. "Eggnog. You've lost your mind."

He rubbed her fingers with his thumb, then turned her hand over, palm up. "Maybe I'll tell your fortune."

"I thought you said your ancestors were pirates, not Gypsies."

"Don't interrupt."

She indulged him, smiling as he studied her hand with fierce concentration.

"You're going to meet a tall, dark stranger," he intoned dramatically, his voice dropping an octave.

"Is this fortune retroactive?" she inquired.

He shot her a withering look. "You're not cooperating."

"The tall, dark stranger has already been met," she pointed out to him.

He waved his free hand dismissively. "All right, all right, don't be such a lawyer. Are you interested in hearing this or not?"

"I'm fascinated," she said. "Riveted."

He glanced up at her again, and she met his gaze with a look of bemused innocence.

"You're going to meet a tall, dark stranger," he began again, "and he will be the most intriguing, unforgettable man you've ever known."

"What a modest Gypsy you are," Morgan said dryly.

"He will sweep you off your feet, and you will find him irresistible," Landry continued as if she hadn't spoken.

"Is this the power of suggestion at work?" Morgan asked archly.

"Subjects having their fortune told are supposed to be quiet," he advised sharply.

"Excuse me."

"Are you ready to hear the rest?"

Morgan squared her shoulders with mock courage.

"You will fall madly in love with him," Landry continued, his tone softening, "and you will be able to refuse him nothing."

"And how will he feel?" Morgan asked quietly.

"The same," Landry answered, abandoning the pretense and raising her hand to his lips. "The very same." He kissed the fleshy mound at the base of her palm, then drew the tip of his tongue across the thin, sensitive skin on the inside of her wrist.

Morgan shivered at the contact. "Is it true?" she whispered.

"It's true," he replied huskily, straightening and drawing her to him. He kissed her lips lightly, teasingly, until she put her hands to the back of his head and forced him closer. Her mouth opened under his willingly as her arms slipped down and around his neck. When he scooped her up and stood with her in his arms she made no protest, letting her head fall back to his shoulder as he carried her into the bedroom.

The fortune-teller was right. She could refuse him nothing.

The bedroom was dimly lit by the dying sunlight filtering through the curtains. Morgan had a fleeting impression of more modern furniture and a king-size brass bed covered by a quilted spread before she found herself upon it, looking up at Landry. He was outlined against the windows, a tall, slim figure in a shadowy room, the object of the most consuming passion she had ever felt.

He reached for the buttons of his shirt and she said, "Don't."

He stopped.

"I'll do that," she said softly.

He moved to sit next to her on the edge of the bed. She couldn't see his expression clearly, but she heard the intake of his breath as she ran her hand inside his collar, slipping the first button from its opening and seeking the warm skin of his chest. She caressed the hard pectoral muscle and the flat nipple, roughened with hair, until he shoved her hand away impatiently.

"Let me take it off," he said hoarsely, tearing at the shirt until she heard the cloth rip. He dropped it on the floor and embraced her in the same motion, his naked skin fiery against her bare arms. She kissed his collar-bone, dragging her lips along the line of his shoulder as he threw his head back and let her make love to him.

She kissed him everywhere she could reach until he finally held her fast, pulling her knit shell over her head with one hand. Her hair tumbled loosely to her shoulders.

"Such beautiful hair," he murmured, touching it lightly. "And it always smells so good."

"Creme rinse," Morgan confessed.

"No," he said. "I think it's just you." He eased her back on the bed and unhooked the front closure of her bra, not pausing to remove it before he separated the scraps of material and cupped one ivory breast in his hand. Morgan gasped as he rubbed the peach-tan nipple with his thumb, raising it to pebble hardness, teasing her until she was tugging on him, trying to pull him down to her.

He bent his head, and she arched toward him, meeting him halfway. His mouth moved from one breast to the other, flooding her skin with wet heat. Morgan held him to her tightly, reveling in the feel of his heavily muscled back under her fingers, the strong column of his neck. Clothing made him appear thinner than he actually was. She slipped her fingers under his belt, putting the flat of her hand against the down at the base of his spine. He responded by moving over her, letting her take his full weight, pressing her back into the mattress. He was fully aroused, hard against her thighs, and she curled her legs around his, unable to get close enough.

"You have the softest, sweetest body," he said into her ear. "You don't know how hard it was for me to hold back the other night at the river."

"Why did you?" she whispered, so besotted with him she was barely able to speak.

"I sensed you weren't ready," he responded, lifting himself on his arms to look down at her.

"And now I am," she murmured.

"I always was," he said huskily. "From the moment we met."

He rolled off her and removed her skirt and the rest of her underwear, pressing his burning cheek to the flat surface of her belly when she was naked. His beard rasped the sensitive skin. She closed her eyes, putting her fist to her mouth as his lips traveled lower, to the inside of her thighs and then to the apex of her legs. Morgan shuddered, mute with pleasure, enduring the delirious sensation until the ache inside her could be denied no longer. She dug her nails into his shoulders, dragging him back.

"What?" he muttered thickly, kissing her abdomen, then the valley between her breasts, working his way upward. "What do you want?"

"You," she whispered. "You, you."

"You got me," he answered, kissing her lips, his mouth dewed and clinging.

"Inside," she moaned. "Inside me."

He sat up, and she hung on to him, her arms about his neck.

"I have to let you go for a moment, baby," he said, half laughing, his voice shaky.

"Why?"

"To take off my pants."

"Well, hurry up," she sighed, and he did, shedding his slacks and shoes in seconds. When he dropped back onto the bed she reached up for him eagerly, and he entered her at once. They both gasped aloud with the sensation.

"Don't stop," Morgan urged as he paused to look down at her. His face was so close that she could see him clearly even in the gathering darkness.

"In a hurry?" he teased, his brown eyes tender.

"Oh, yes," she answered. "I've been waiting for you such a long time. I have a lot to make up for, Beau."

"Me, too," he replied, and then showed her that he meant it.

When Morgan woke she didn't realize where she was at first. She started, looking around at the darkened, unfamiliar room, and then the weight of Landry's arm across her middle reminded her of what had happened.

She tugged the sheet back from her bare breasts, wondering what time it was. Landry was sleeping next to her, face down, one leg thrown across hers. She disentangled herself gently, moving his arm and sliding her leg from under his. He stirred but didn't waken.

She stretched contentedly, luxuriously satiated, and sat naked on the edge of the bed, looking around for something to wear. Her clothes were scattered and wrinkled and she didn't feel like straightening out the mess. She spotted Landry's torn shirt on the floor and retrieved it, then slipped it on and buttoned it. It fit her like a tent but at least she was covered.

Landry sighed and snuggled deeper into his pillow. Morgan traced his spine lightly with a tentative forefinger, almost unable to believe that she had just slept with him. God, he was beautiful. His tanned torso stood out in bas relief against the white sheets, perfectly formed, the cotton blanket twisted down to his waist.

Can I be this lucky? Morgan wondered. Was it really possible to live the dream, be Cinderella without the wicked stepmother, Sleeping Beauty without the forest of briers? Was there no poisoned apple in this fairy tale? So far she hadn't found one.

She slipped off the bed and padded barefoot into the living room, where the clock on the fireplace mantel told her it was after midnight. She thought of Julie and looked for the telephone. She found it on the kitchen wall, and went back to the bedroom to close the door before she placed her call. She didn't want to disturb her lover.

Julie answered on the first ring.

"Hi, it's me," Morgan said.

"Where the hell are you?" Julie demanded.

"At Beau's apartment," Morgan replied.

"And what are you doing there? Playing ticktacktoe, I suppose?"

"Not exactly."

"Morgan, are you telling me what I think you're telling me?"

"I guess so."

"You wound up in bed, right?"

"Right."

There was a loud sigh from the other end of the line. Then, "Oh, boy. This is getting complicated."

"Tell me about it."

"Not that I blame you. That guy wouldn't have to ask me twice. But I gather we're not going to be telling Gorgeous Jerry Sinclair about this latest development."

"It's none of his—"

"...business. Yes, I know," Julie said, interrupting. "And speaking of business, we're supposed to be getting back to it in the morning. I trust you'll be here?"

"I'll be there."

"Sure you can tear yourself away from that devastating creature long enough to get your work done?"

"Meow. Sounds like jealousy to me."

"You're so right. Well, don't let me keep you. I'm sure you have more interesting things to do than talk to your poor, love-starved friend on the phone. I'll see you in the morning?"

"I'll be back early."

"Hah. You'll be back late, if you're back at all. That's all right, don't give it a second thought. Kiss him for me, will you?"

"I will."

"Good night," Julie said.

"Bye." Morgan hung up the phone, smiling to herself. Julie was a character. Her acid tongue disguised a generous nature. She was probably as happy about Morgan's good fortune as Morgan was herself.

The air conditioning condenser switched on automatically, sounding loud in the quiet apartment. Morgan's stomach growled ominously for accompaniment, and she opened the refrigerator. She spotted a lone apple inside, partially hidden among several bottles of mixers, a carton of eggs, two wedges of hardening cheese and a wilting head of lettuce. Landry was apparently a frequent patronizer of restaurants. She grabbed the apple and was taking a bite of it, turning away, when a notepad fixed to the metal door with a magnet caught her eye.

"Call M. Aguilar," it said in Landry's handwriting. "Discuss split."

Aguilar, Morgan thought. The name sounded familiar. Why? She was wandering back to the living room, thinking, when it came to her.

Juan Aguilar was one of the deceased oil workers in the Sunlite case. Maria Aguilar was his wife, a plaintiff. Morgan was scheduled to interview her the next week.

Why would Landry be calling her? His part in the Sunlite case was finished. And to discuss a 'split'? Was that some sort of oil industry term she didn't recognize?

She was sitting on the gray sofa, munching the apple and puzzling about it, when Landry appeared from the bedroom, zipping the fly of his gray pants.

"Ah-ha," he said when he saw her. "Midnight raids on the refrigerator? Is this one of those bad habits a guy only finds out about afterward?"

"There's precious little to raid in your refrigerator, buddy," Morgan replied. "Where have you been eating dinner, the local hot dog stand?"

"I like the pizza joint, too," he said, grinning.

"What woke you up?" she asked.

"I heard a little mouse out here, scrabbling around for a piece of cheese."

"No self-respecting mouse would have your cheese, Beauregarde. It's growing mold."

He sauntered over to her and kissed the top of her head. "I can make scrambled eggs," he said.

"Anything else?"

"Hard-boiled eggs, soft-boiled eggs, eggs over easy, sunnyside up...."

Morgan held up a hand. "I get the picture. Scrambled eggs will be fine."

He went into the kitchen and she got up to dispose of her apple core. As she walked past him to the wastebasket, his arm snaked out and he pulled her against him.

"Mmm," he said, nuzzling her. "You smell like me."

"I'm not surprised," she answered, rubbing her nose against his shoulder.

"And I like that outfit," he added, releasing her and opening a cabinet to remove a frying pan. "It displays those gorgeous legs."

"And it comes with ventilation," Morgan observed, putting her hand through the rent in the front of the shirt.

"I guess we got a little carried away," he said, looking over his shoulder at her and smiling.

She smiled back. Their eyes met and held.

He put down the pan and hugged her, rocking her back and forth. "Would you like to get carried away again?" he murmured, biting the shell of her ear gently.

"Sounds like a great idea," she sighed, closing her eyes.

"I thought you were hungry."

"Not for food," she said, and he turned her toward the bedroom, taking her hand.

"Then come with me," he said huskily. "I think I can take care of your problem."

Morgan followed where he led.

She had forgotten the note on the refrigerator.

Eight

For the next two weeks Morgan worked on the Sunlite
case by day and saw Beau Landry during every moment
of her free time. He took her to see Belle Isle—by car, via
the road—and it was every bit as impressive as advertised, a rolling spread of bottom land on a bluff overlooking the river. Only the foundation of the rebuilt
house was in place, but Morgan could see from the plans
that it would be a showplace as grand as the original
when completed. They toured the jazz clubs and ate at
Landry's favorite restaurants—Morgan drew the line at
any more Cajun fireworks, but Landry was careful to
make sure her choices were conservative. She saw his
hometown through his eyes and fell in love with New
Orleans as she had fallen in love with him.

Morgan was happier than she had ever been in her life.

One day late into the second week of her stay Morgan
was preparing a packet of progress reports to send to

Jerry Sinclair. She had wrapped up her interviews the previous afternoon. Although Landry was the only witness who could testify to legal negligence, she was hoping the other depositions were clear enough on the subject of Sunlite's careless practices to convince Sinclair to settle out of court. She was attaching a cover letter to that effect.

"I wish the Perez boy or Mrs. Gutierrez had been able to confirm what Landry said directly," Julie observed from the bed, giving voice to the nagging concern clouding Morgan's mind. "I'd feel better if the whole case weren't resting on Landry and that Aguilar woman. He's only one person, and she's a very interested party. Even she admits she wouldn't have known a code violation if she saw one. A judge isn't going to be too comfortable with her 'feelings' and 'beliefs.' They're all suppositions."

"She's very religious," Morgan answered. "She was so concerned about saying something that might be misinterpreted she wound up qualifying every word that came out of her mouth."

"I guess your boyfriend doesn't have that problem, huh?" Julie said.

Morgan looked up at her sharply. "What's that supposed to mean?"

Julie shrugged. "Merely that he's the only one who's sure of anything. Without him we've got no case, just a lot of meandering about what a rotten, money-grubbing outfit Sunlite is. That won't hold up in court."

"Julie, are you in any doubt that Sunlite was in the wrong?" Morgan asked directly.

"No, of course not. But I don't have to tell you that knowing it is a far cry from being able to prove it."

Morgan was silent, thinking.

"Well?" Julie said.

"You're right. We're relying on the testimony of one witness and our own personal observations to make the recommendation to settle," Morgan agreed. "But I can't think what else to do. Beau would kill us in court, you know that. He's rational and credible and very articulate."

"Spoken like a woman who's in love with him," Julie said stoutly.

"It's the truth. He'd have any judge believing that Sunlite was the most negligent employer since the sweatshops, and I don't have to tell you what he'd do to a jury. He'd tell a story that would make the 1890s garment district look benevolent by comparison with our beloved insured."

"You don't have to convince me. I agree with you," Julie grumbled. "Let's just hope that Generous Jerry never finds out that you were sleeping with the star witness."

Morgan winced. "Do you have to put it that way?"

Julie blinked ingenuously. "I beg your pardon. What are you doing with him? Outlining a plan for world peace?"

Morgan shoved a sheaf of papers into an envelope and licked the inside of the flap. "Sometimes you can really be a pain, Julie," she muttered, sealing the envelope expertly.

Julie flopped back on the bed and stared at the ceiling. "Don't mind me, I'm just crazed with envy. You come to New Orleans and snag that fine specimen of manhood. I come to New Orleans and get a heat rash. It just isn't fair. Every night that you spend with him I lie here by myself and dwell on the inequities of life. Beginning with the fact that you got the blond hair and blue eyes, and I got the washed out red-brown-whatever-it-is and the lashless, colorless duo stuck here in the middle of my face."

"Julie, that is absurd," Morgan said, laughing. "You know you're very attractive."

"Then why isn't Mr. Beauregarde Landry lusting after me?" Julie inquired reasonably.

"Because I met him first," Morgan replied.

"Humph," Julie said. "That's very nice of you to say, but neither of us believes it. I may get so hard up I'll go back to the City of Brotherly Love and throw myself into the arms of our illustrious leader."

"You'll never be lonely enough to make Jerry look good," Morgan said. "I'm glad I won't be around when he opens up this package." She printed the express mail label carefully, leaning on the pen to make clear copies.

"When are you telling him we'll be back?" Julie asked.

"I'm leaving that open. I'm sure he'll call when he gets this, if only to express his disappointment loudly and in no uncertain terms over long distance."

"You don't want to go back, do you?" Julie said quietly.

Morgan stood and put the package addressed to her boss on the nightstand. "I can't say I'm anxious to leave Beau, no. But he's planning to come and visit me in Philly in a couple of weeks, so I won't be missing him for too long."

"He said he'd come to see you up north?" Julie asked.

"Yes."

"He must be really serious about you, Morgan," Julie said wonderingly.

"I hope so," Morgan replied.

"Do you think you'll marry him?" Julie inquired, wide-eyed. She hadn't realized that the affair had moved so quickly to this stage.

"If he asks me, I will."

"And live down here?" Julie asked, horrified. She hated the heat so much that in her mind moving to the Mississippi river basin was like volunteering for a permanent sentence to purgatory.

"I'm getting to like it," Morgan replied. "I could practice here. I would have to brush up on the Napoleonic code, of course. Or I could take the bar across the river in Mississippi, they have common law just like Pennsylvania."

"I see. So you've been giving this a lot of thought."

"Some, yes."

"Just waiting for him to pop the question, to use a phrase of my mother's that I've always hated?"

Julie's expression was so miserable that Morgan moved to sit next to her on the bed.

"What is it?" she asked.

"I'll miss you," Julie said in a small voice.

"We'll see each other. As far as I know the planes and trains are still running."

"You'll be leaving me to deal with Jerry all by myself."

"You can handle him."

"Easy for you to say. You'll be playing footsie with your good-looking tootsie while I'm trying to convince Jerry to fork over enough cash to put me up in a Holiday Inn instead of the usual Ranchero Roacho."

Morgan collapsed on the bed in hysterics. "Could you repeat that, please?" she gasped when she was able to talk.

"You heard me," Julie observed morosely. "That's what his name means, you know."

"Whose name?" Morgan asked weakly, wiping her eyes.

"Beau's. Beauregarde. It means 'good looking' in French."

"You know, you're right," Morgan said in surprise, sitting up. "I never thought of that."

"Not that you haven't observed the accuracy of the nomenclature," Julie said pompously.

"Where's the dictionary?" Morgan said, grinning.

"Ha-ha. What time is old Beauregarde picking you up?" Julie asked.

Morgan glanced at her watch. "In about fifteen minutes."

"Where are you going tonight?"

"Just to his apartment."

"For an intense discussion of the nuclear arms race, I assume," Julie said tartly.

Morgan threw a pillow at her.

"Be sure to take notes," Julie added.

"What!"

"I'll want to hear all about his theories on the deployment of MX missiles."

"Julie . . ."

"Yeah, I know. Wash my hair, do my nails. I now have the cleanest head south of the Mason-Dixon line and my cuticles are peeling. But have a great time, really. Don't give me a second thought." She vaulted off the bed and headed for the hall, calling back, "I'm just going to get some ice from the machine downstairs. I'll try to drown my sorrows in Orange Crush." The door slammed behind her.

Morgan was still smiling to herself as she went into the bathroom to change.

"What's for dinner?" Morgan asked as she followed Beau into his apartment. "Something smells good."

"Veal parmigiana."

Morgan stared at him as he went to the oven door and peered in the glass window. "You actually cooked something?" she asked incredulously.

"Take-out from the Italian restaurant on Carnival Street," he replied. "The lady there gave me instructions on how to reheat it."

"Whew," Morgan said, fanning herself. "I had a bad moment there, almost passed out from the shock."

"Everybody's a comedian," he muttered, turning down the oven temperature. "Since you're no better in the kitchen than I am, I wonder at your sense of humor on the subject."

"I spent seven years in college, what's your excuse?"

"Pulling rank on me?" he demanded, lunging for her. She danced into the living room, out of his reach. But he was too fast; he caught her about the waist and spun her back to him, wrestling her to the floor. Morgan was laughing too hard to put up an effective resistance, flailing her hands futilely.

"Before you get cute," he said, pinning her arms with ease, "just remember who outweighs who by sixty pounds."

"Sixty-two."

"I stand corrected. And who is taller by seven inches?"

"You are."

He was half lying across her, looking down into her face. "Then we're clear about who's going to come out on top in this contest?"

"You're already on top," she pointed out calmly. "And I think your veal is burning."

"I put it on 'keep warm.'"

"If you leave it on 'keep warm' too long you'll be able to play racquetball with it."

"Ah, the hell with dinner," he said, unbuttoning her blouse. "We'll have peanut butter and jelly sandwiches later."

"We had peanut butter and jelly sandwiches last night. I feel like I'm in third grade. Pretty soon I'm going to be carrying a Gobots lunch box and asking for a pass to go to the bathroom."

"You're very well developed for a third grader," Landry said, kissing the tip of her left breast.

"It's all those Flintstones vitamins."

"Did I ever tell you how happy I am that they moved these little hooks around to the front?" he asked, unhooking deftly. "What a wonderful idea."

"They're not always in the front, Beau," Morgan said, trying to reply clearly and ignore what he was doing. "I just buy that style."

"Clever girl." He was removing articles of her clothing rapidly, humming under his breath.

"Beau, can't we go into the bedroom?" Morgan inquired faintly, already too enervated to move.

"Nope. I thought you liked this rug."

"I like it fine, but not for . . ." She gasped, closing her eyes as he put his tongue in her navel.

"For?" he whispered, sliding his hands up her thighs.

"What you're doing," she sighed.

"Shall I stop?" he muttered, pulling her into the cradle of his hips. "Shall I?"

"No, no," she said fiercely, pulling him down to her and kissing him wildly.

He kissed her back, and she stopped thinking about the rug, or anything else.

The telephone rang the next day when Morgan was alone in her hotel room. Julie had gone to file some preliminary papers at the parish courthouse, and Morgan lifted the receiver distractedly, thinking that Julie wanted to check something with her.

"Hello?" she said.

"Morgan? It's Jerry," came the greeting from the other end of the line.

Morgan sat up straight. "Hi, Jerry."

"I've been going over the file you sent me yesterday," Jerry said, never one to beat about the bush. Not at long-distance phone rates, anyway.

"Yes? I think it's self-explanatory," Morgan said.

"Only if this guy Landry is solid gold. And I'm not sure we should go with his testimony."

Morgan's fingers tightened on the receiver. "Why not?"

"Well, when I saw that the whole question turned on what he had to say, I decided to do some checking on him."

"I checked on him. He's well respected in the community, has a clean business record. His family is Old South, bloodlines go way back."

Sinclair made a disgusted sound. "Don't be snowed by that Southern gentry bull. I'm talking about would he lie to get what he wants from this case. And I think he would."

"How does he stand to gain? He's not even a plaintiff."

"He stands to gain," Sinclair replied smugly.

"Explain," Morgan said tersely. She could only trust herself to one word.

"Well, first of all, are you aware that the guy almost went bankrupt last year when the oil drilling trickled to nothing? His business was locating reservoirs."

"He diversified," Morgan said, trying to keep her voice steady.

"Not before he borrowed everything but grandma's buggy to keep going. He's mortgaged to the eyeballs, got paper out all over the state."

"So what? He's turning things around now. As long as he meets his notes nobody complains. Being in debt doesn't make him a perjured witness."

"Lying to make sure the plaintiffs win the Sunlite case does," Sinclair said.

Morgan sat down. Her legs were shaking. "What are you talking about?"

Sinclair sighed with exaggerated patience, as if attempting to converse with a backward kindergartner. "Look, the guy needs money. He's got multiple mortgages, plus he's trying to restore the family homestead or some damn thing, right?"

"How do you know all this?"

"I'll get to that in a minute. So he strikes a deal. He's the perfect witness, the geophysicist with the expert lingo to impress a jury, and disinterested, not a party to the suit, not even an employee of Sunlite. You follow me so far? He goes to the plaintiffs and says, 'I'll lie like a rug to get you the dough, and then afterward we split it.' They carve it up six ways instead of five; they still walk away with, what, three quarters of a mil each on the proposed settlement? How does that sound?"

Morgan's mouth was dry. She couldn't speak.

"Taylor? You there?"

Morgan wet her lips. "Yes," she said softly.

"It's foolproof. He convinced you. He would certainly convince a jury. My source tells me this guy Landry is a real charmer—pretty for the ladies, macho for the men. If it went to trial, goodbye Sunlite, but he wasn't even taking that chance. He made sure it would never go to trial by sandbagging you. So much easier to get us to settle. Quick and easy. Take the money and run."

"Who is your source?" Morgan asked. Her voice sounded strange to her own ears, distant and hollow.

"One of the attorney's at Sunlite. He's local down there, got an in with the banks and credit institutions, has access to confidential information you couldn't pry loose with a crowbar. I worked with him preparing the case, and when I saw Landry figuring so prominently in your decision to settle I thought I'd better get the lowdown on him. Interesting, huh?"

Good for you, Jerry, Morgan thought dully. You did your job, better than I did mine. But then, you're not in love with Beau Landry.

"Well, what do you think?" Sinclair asked.

Morgan cleared her throat. "I think you may have a point," she said quietly.

"Good, good. You said in your letter that Landry was the only one willing to testify to legal negligence, and that bothered you. It bothered the hell out of me, too, and now you can see why. The other witnesses are telling the truth; Landry is spinning yarns. Sunlite may be dirty as hell, but it wasn't violating the law. Landry wants to nail the company. He knows the law, so he's making up specifics. The other witnesses don't have them because they don't exist. Make sense?"

"It makes sense," Morgan said. The knuckles of her hand gripping the receiver were white.

"We've got the method—Landry's imaginative mouth—and the motive—filthy lucre. What more do you want?" Sinclair asked triumphantly.

"Those people are still dead because Sunlite was running a dirty show, Jerry," Morgan said.

Sinclair snorted. "What, I have to teach you the basics now? If Sunlite's legal, it's home free. It could be responsible for the mass murder of millions and if the conduct is clean, it walks. That's all you need to know."

"That's all I need to know," Morgan echoed.

"Taylor, you okay?" Sinclair asked. "You sound kind of . . . funny."

"I'm fine," Morgan lied.

"So, how do we handle it?" Sinclair asked. "Do you confront him now and knock him out of the box, or do we take him into court and discredit him there?"

"It won't be as easy as you think to discredit him," Morgan said evenly. "He's very . . . persuasive."

"A fancy dancer, eh?"

"Yes."

"Could he handle a cross, redirect?"

"I think so. He's very smart." Smart enough to con a very smart lady. One who used to think she was smart, anyway.

"Then get him to retract now. Can you handle it?"

"I can handle it."

"All right. Let me know how it goes. And Taylor?"

"Yes?"

"Don't feel bad about missing the boat on Landry. You couldn't have dug up this dirt. I'll owe the Sunlite guy my first-born son for passing on the stuff. You know how touchy banks are about their records; they release loan reports only on a written request from God."

"Thanks, Jerry." Morgan stared at the pattern on the hotel room rug. This was some time for Jerry Sinclair to show a touch of common decency. He was human after all, and her beloved Beau Landry was a crook. What a world.

"Keep in touch," Sinclair said, and hung up. Morgan replaced the receiver and then gazed numbly at the phone. He was leaving the case in her hands. She was surely the dumbest blonde since *Born Yesterday* and Jerry Sinclair had faith in her. He didn't blame her for this screwup, he thought it was only his access to superior information that had made the difference.

It was certainly farcical, but she didn't feel very much like laughing.

Unbidden and fully formed, like Athena from the brow of Zeus, a vision of the note on Landry's refrigerator rose before her.

"Call M. Aguilar. Discuss split."

Maria Aguilar, the plaintiff who'd been so nervous when interviewed, so careful about what she said.

Morgan now knew why the woman was nervous. And what split Landry had been calling her to "discuss."

You're a slick article, Beau Landry, she said to herself. Too slippery by half. You had me fooled, all right. Of course you didn't have to carry it as far as you did, making love to me, holding out the promise of a future together, but after all, why not? Nothing like a little sex to seal the deal. And after you got the money, what then? A change of heart. Maybe an "I'm not ready" speech, or a "we should see other people" lecture. That was always good. Anything to ditch the unwanted encumbrance once the check was in hand.

Morgan bit her lip, not feeling the pain. You told the truth about one thing, Beau. Success and the restoration of your family name are very important to you. So important that you'd use me or anybody else to achieve them.

Brilliant, Beau. A masterful plan from a masterful planner.

A single tear was stealing down Morgan's cheek, and she swiped at it impatiently. She had things to do.

She picked up the phone purposefully and dialed Landry's office. When Yvonne Hastings answered, Morgan asked to speak to him, and the secretary complied.

Her boss had instructed her that Morgan's calls were always to be put through immediately.

"Hey, *chère*," Beau said warmly when he came on the line. "Miss me?"

Morgan almost lost it when she heard his voice. She gritted her teeth and swallowed a sob before saying, in an approximation of her normal voice, "Beau, can we meet for lunch?"

"Sure, any time you like. I thought you were going to be busy today."

"Something came up. Your apartment okay?"

"The food is better at Gino's," he said jokingly, naming a place they often went for lunch.

"I'd like to keep it private."

He heard the note of controlled panic she was trying to hide and said quickly, "Morgan, is anything wrong?"

"I'll tell you about it when I see you. Twelve-thirty at your place." She hung up before he could reply, grabbed her briefcase with her paperwork inside it, and bolted from the room before the phone could ring.

Nine

Morgan was waiting for Landry outside his door when he stepped off the elevator. He stopped short, then glanced at his watch.

"You got here pretty fast," he greeted her.

Morgan said nothing, standing to one side as he unlocked his door.

Once in the apartment he turned to her immediately.

"All right," he said flatly. "What's wrong?"

Morgan met his eyes. He was watching her with an expression she had never seen before, tense and speculative. This was the Beau Landry who could lie to the woman he was supposed to love: a sharp-eyed, sharp-witted stranger.

Morgan opened her briefcase on the kitchen table and pulled out a copy of his deposition.

"Recognize this?" she said, handing it to him.

He glanced down briefly at the cover page as he took it, then looked up at her.

"Of course, Morgan. Will you please tell me what's going on?"

"Is that a true copy of your testimony to me at the day and time listed?"

He shrugged. "Yes, I suppose so."

"Would you like to look it over and make sure of that?"

He tossed the deposition back on the table and seized her by her upper arms with bruising strength. She winced, and he lessened his grip.

"Tell me," he said curtly. "Now."

Morgan pulled back from him until he was forced to release her or hold her against her will. He released her.

"I had an interesting phone call from my superior at TA today," she said, walking away, turning her back on him. "He told me quite a bit about your financial situation."

Landry stared at her. "My financial situation?"

Morgan nodded. "Your loans, outstanding mortgages, the state of your business affairs."

Landry's mouth hardened. "How would your boss know about my business affairs?" he asked coldly.

"Never mind that for the moment. Is it true that you're heavily in debt, that you almost went under last year?"

He turned his head, his eyes shifting from her face. "I told you about that," he said shortly. "I told you I had to find other business when the oil boom went bust. I went through a tough period during the transition with nothing coming in except bills. I had just bought this place when the trouble began and I had to take a second lien on it, encumber some of the rigs and other equipment with chattel mortgages. But I learned from the ex-

perience not to base my whole business on one enterprise.
It's turned around now and things are picking up again."
He put his hands on his hips and faced her down. "What
does my financial picture have to do with that deposition or this weirdo act you're putting on? I'm not a witness you're trying to intimidate, Morgan, you'd better
explain yourself."

"I think you're going to be doing the explaining,
Beau," Morgan said quietly.

He waited, wisely saying nothing, his dark eyes fixed
on her face. He had never looked better to her, more de-
sirable. Morgan stiffened her spine.

"You must still require quite a bit of cash to cover your
loans," she said quietly.

"I'm paying them off," he responded. "Get to the
point."

"The point is that you need money. A lot of it."

His eyes widened. "I am *making* money. A lot of it.
Do you want to see my receipts for the last six months?
We'll go back to my office right now."

"That won't be necessary."

"Morgan, what the hell is this?" he demanded fiercely.
"I resent this damn interrogation. I'll tell you anything
you want to know but I don't like having to defend myself against allegations I haven't even heard."

Morgan pointed to the refrigerator door. His eyes followed her hand, his expression bewildered.

"The first night I came here, the first time we made
love...." Her voice faltered, and his eyes softened.

"That night," she continued, "while you were still
sleeping, I came out here and saw a note on that refrigerator door."

His gaze was still uncomprehending.

"I got up to call Julie and then had an apple, remember? I saw a little slip of paper fixed to the door with one of those magnetic things. It said, 'Call M. Aguilar. Discuss split.'"

His eyes flickered.

"I recognized the name," she went on, walking around the table, "but I couldn't put it together. Then when I interviewed Maria Aguilar she was a gibbering wreck. Depositions sometimes make people nervous, Beau, but that woman was almost in tears. It seemed an excessive reaction then, but now I know why she was so upset. She was trying to tell the truth, as her conscience dictated, and still stay within the guidelines of your coaching. You set her quite a task, my friend."

He lifted his chin a fraction, his lips parting.

Morgan took a step toward him. "You badgered that poor woman into going along with you, but she was too moral to actually lie outright. God knows you don't have that problem."

"Now wait a minute..." he began.

"Shut up," she snapped, and he flinched visibly.

"What did you tell her?" Morgan demanded. "What kind of a 'split' did you promise her? She's got a dead husband and six kids she can't support. I guess she didn't require that much persuasion, but you would have been equal to the job even if she had. I'm living proof that you could sell ice skates to Tahitians if you wanted to do it."

"Morgan, listen to me..." he said quickly.

"No," she said firmly, picking up the deposition and holding it before her. "I have already listened to *you*, thank you very much. And the result was *this* pack of lies." She threw the document in his face.

He struck it to the floor, moving to reach her. Morgan put out her hands.

"Don't you touch me," she said warningly.

He fell back, buying time, trying to judge how to handle her.

"You know," she said in a baffled tone, "I couldn't determine why, out of all the people I interviewed, each of whom agreed that Sunlite was careless and responsible for the accident, only you had every little detail, every incident that would put the company away. A cretin could have figured it out in a minute, of course. It took my boss about ten seconds." She shook her head. "But I had this tiny problem, you see. I believed *you*."

"Morgan, Sunlite *was* responsible for the accident; the operation was a mess. That company killed those people as surely as if its president had lined them up and shot them. All I did was make certain that Sunlite would be held responsible in court for those deaths."

Morgan drew a deep breath. "So you admit that you manufactured those incidents you described in the deposition?"

He studied her for a moment, then released his breath explosively, his shoulders dropping. "Yes."

"To collect a portion of the settlement from the plaintiffs, who wouldn't have gotten a dime without your testimony."

His mouth fell open, his eyes widening. "What? No! Where did you get that idea?"

"You might say it occurred to me when I found out that you owed everybody from the federal government to the local dry-cleaner. The notion was not discouraged by the vivid memory of the 'split' you were planning to discuss with Mrs. Aguilar."

"Now just hang on there," he said, shaking his head. "Any settlement was going to be divided up among the families. We were just going to talk about who was getting how much, depending on the number of kids, educational needs, things like that. I wasn't going to take one cent, Morgan, I swear to God.''

"Aren't you noble?" she said sarcastically. "A liar, but a noble one. Do you actually expect me to credit one word that you say now?"

"Ask Maria Aguilar," he said simply. "You know she'll tell you the truth. I set it up for them to recover with the testimony I gave you, but not for a cut of the money."

"Then why?"

"Juan Aguilar was my friend," he replied gently. "I worked with him for years. I knew all of the dead men. I wanted their families to have something. No power on earth can bring their husbands and fathers back, but the money would help a lot for the future. I just couldn't stand by and watch another big company, with a team of insurance lawyers ready to pounce on any technicality, get away with murder. Not when I could do something about it."

"You lied under oath," Morgan said flatly. "You could be prosecuted."

"Are you going to do it?"

"I don't have to do anything. You're going to retract that deposition or I'll put you on the witness stand and tear you down to nothing. I might even get up there myself and repeat what you just told me. Where would that leave your friends? I'll tell you. Without a penny of the money that you, of course, were not going to share in at all."

He eyed her levelly. "You don't believe me about that?" he asked.

"I'm supposed to believe you lied about the one thing and not the other?" she countered.

"Yes, yes!" he said. "What do I care if Sunlite Petroleum, or Trans-whatever, forks over several million bucks to people who actually deserve to get it? Companies like that have a hundred billion more where that came from. What's the price of human life, Morgan?"

"A liar is a liar," she said distantly, not looking at him. "You can't make me subscribe to this gentleman-bandit philosophy. Wrong is wrong."

"Is that what you really think?" he asked incredulously. "Can't you see the difference? Is your whole world so black and white? I didn't do it for money, *chère*. I did it to help some people I care about who needed the help. I can make my own money. I'm making it right now. In a year or so I'll be free and clear; I don't have to take Sunlite for a ride to get where I want to go."

She gazed at him stonily, refusing to concede his point.

"You know as well as I do that Sunlite deserves to pay, and pay dearly, for that accident," he said. "All the rest is a dispute over trifles."

"It's not my job to make judgments like that. I work within the system," Morgan replied stiffly. "You would best be advised to do the same, or you could wind up behind bars, where, based on this incident, I'm becoming convinced you belong." She picked up the deposition from the floor, tossed it into her briefcase, and dropped the lid, snapping the hasps closed smartly.

He watched her, unable to comprehend her intransigence. His reasoning made perfect sense to him.

"Where are you going?" he asked.

"Back to Philadelphia," she replied. "Where I am going to recommend that TA go to court to defend the Sunlite case. I expect to win handily."

He nodded wearily, defeated. There was a short silence before he said, "Don't you care that you're on the wrong side in this? Don't you care that all those families will be left penniless because your client's negligence killed off the breadwinners?''

She eyed him narrowly. ''Don't try to put this back on me, Beau. I didn't perjure myself, you did. You don't like the probable outcome here? Maybe I don't, either. But I'm not ready to throw away the rule book and go back to vigilante justice.'' She picked up her briefcase with one hand and shouldered her purse with the other.

''Morgan, wait,'' he said.

She kept walking toward the door.

''We're not finished,'' he said, blocking her path.

''Yes, we are.'' She waited for him to move.

A long pause ensued, during which they eyed each other warily.

''This isn't really about Sunlite at all, is it?'' he finally said thoughtfully.

''Please get out of the way,'' she said, ignoring him. ''I have a lot to do this afternoon.''

''Oh, you're angry about the case, all right,'' he went on as if she hadn't spoken, ''but you're more upset about us.''

''Us?'' she said scornfully. ''There is no 'us.' You used me to get what you wanted. You thought that if you made love to me, convinced me that you cared about me, I would be easier to fool. And you were right.''

''For God's sake, Morgan, that is ridiculous,'' he said, taking her by the shoulders. ''I meant everything I said to you about our relationship.''

''And I should believe *you*, of course,'' she said. ''Your track record for veracity is impeccable.''

He threw up his hands in frustration. ''I do one thing you don't approve of and all of a sudden every syllable I've ever uttered is a lie?''

"You said it, I didn't. And the 'one thing' you did wasn't minor, Mr. Landry. Now, do I have to call security in order to get out of this apartment?"

"Morgan, don't do this," he said softly. He took her chin in his hand. She jerked her head away, but she could feel the sting of tears beginning in her eyes.

"Are you really going to walk out on me without a backward glance?" he asked huskily.

"Let me go," she murmured, her lower lip trembling. He kissed it.

Morgan resisted, pulling back from him. "That won't work this time, Beau. You took advantage of my trust, of the way I felt about you." She closed her eyes, the tears running down her cheeks. "You made me believe you loved me," she added in a whisper.

"I do love you," he said hoarsely. "That has nothing to do with the Sunlite case, and it won't change. Ever."

She turned her head from side to side blindly, wiping her cheeks with the back of her hand. "I'm not going to listen to you anymore," she sobbed. "I'm not. You'll just confuse me again."

"Morgan, will you be sensible?" he said sternly, trying another tack. "Stop acting like a betrayed woman and think like the lawyer you're supposed to be. I didn't falsify that deposition to hurt your feelings or outsmart you in any way. I did it for what I thought was good and sufficient reason, and if you can't see that, fine. But don't let it spoil things between us."

"It has spoiled them," she said tremulously, blinking to clear her vision. "I can't put feelings and experiences into neat, separate compartments that way. You gave false testimony in the Sunlite case, you did it for money, and you don't love me. Goodbye."

He searched her face, and then, seeing that she couldn't be moved, he stepped aside. He listened as she went to the door, then through it, sagging against the wall when she was gone. He drew a deep, tortuous breath, and it caught in the middle, like a sob.

Out in the hall Morgan stopped before the elevator, trying to find the button through a blur of tears. She punched the wrong one and sent the damn thing down and up again before getting on, looking over her shoulder to make sure Landry was not coming after her.

He wasn't.

Morgan was lying on the bed in her hotel room, staring at the ceiling, when Julie burst through the door, singing.

"'Got along without you before I met you, gonna get along without you now,'" she yodeled, twirling past the mirror.

Great choice of tunes, Morgan thought. Keep singing.

Julie spotted her on the bed. "You're not going to believe this," she announced.

"Oh, I don't know, try me," Morgan said dully. "Experience has shown that I will believe anything."

Puzzled by her manner, but too excited to dwell on it, Julie announced, "I have a date." She bowed with a flourish, like an Elizabethan cavalier.

Morgan sat up. "With whom?"

"One of the assistant D.A.'s in the Vieux Carré district. I met him in the sessions clerk's office when I was filing those papers. He took me to lunch and then asked me out for tonight."

It sounded like Julie's lunch hour had gone better than Morgan's. "That's great, Julie," Morgan said, trying to appear enthusiastic.

Julie sat on the bed, kicking off her shoes. "Am I mistaken or are you less than transported by my news?" she asked dryly.

Morgan rolled over and turned her face into the pillow. "I'm happy for you, Julie," she mumbled. "Really."

"Then why the gloom and doom atmosphere? Is there a body in the bathroom?"

"I had kind of a bad day," Morgan said.

"Could you speak up? You sound like you're talking through marshmallow fluff."

Morgan turned again, propping her chin in her hand and tossing the pillow onto the floor. "Bad day," she repeated.

"How so?"

Morgan sighed. "Have you got time?"

Julie glanced at her watch. "Bob isn't coming until seven. What is it?"

"It's about the Sunlite case. We're going to change our strategy. I've already spoken to Jerry about it."

"Why the change?"

Morgan met Julie's eyes. "There is no direct evidence of legal negligence. Beau was lying about all of it. He made up everything that he told me."

Julie stared at her. "Are you kidding me?" she said slowly.

Morgan smiled bitterly. "Do I look like I'm kidding?"

"He admitted that to you?"

"Yes. Under duress, of course, but the end result is the same. We don't have to settle at all. We can take the case to court and win."

"Jerry will be real happy about that," Julie said cautiously.

"You bet."

"Okay," Julie sighed, folding her arms. "Tell me all about it."

Morgan did, sparing none of the gory details. Julie listened in appalled silence, not even interrupting with questions until Morgan's voice ran down like a clockwork monkey and there was nothing left to say.

"How awful for you," Julie finally murmured softly.

"But good for the case, you have to admit," Morgan said.

"Oh, screw the case," Julie said. "TA and Sunlite will survive. I'm not sure you will."

"I feel like such a fool," Morgan said. "I don't know whether to laugh or cry or go bowling."

"From what I remember of your performance in the bar association tournament last year, bowling's out."

Morgan managed a feeble smile.

"That's better. So. How are you feeling about all of this now?"

"Drained. I still can't believe it. All along I thought he was too good to be true, and you see? I was right. He was."

"Morgan, how could you have known? You didn't do anything wrong."

"Except believe in the wrong man." She gestured disgustedly. "You should have seen him, Julie. Even after he admitted that he lied on the deposition he was still trying to tell me that he had only done it for a good cause and that he wasn't going to keep any of the money. And that he loves me, I shouldn't leave that out." She shook her head. "The man is obviously convinced that he can get me to swallow anything."

"Do you think that much could be true?" Julie asked.

"What?"

"That he really just wanted the plaintiffs to recover?"

Morgan looked at her. "So what? It doesn't justify what he did."

"It hardly makes him as guilty as the picture you're painting."

"Are you taking his part now?" Morgan asked, outraged.

"Of course not. I'm merely saying that his version is reasonable from a certain point of view and—"

"Not from mine. I'm the person he's been leading down the garden path for the last three weeks."

"He could still care about you," Julie said quietly.

"Oh, please." Morgan lay flat on the bed with her arms folded over her head. "I will not be able to stand it if you start sounding like him."

"Morgan, listen. He probably decided to lie about Sunlite's case long before he ever met you. He would have told the same story to whoever showed up, to get the plaintiffs a settlement. He didn't know how things were going to be with you in the future. You took that deposition from him when you first met him, right?"

"Julie, this isn't making me feel any better. Are you telling me I should be happy because maybe he isn't a creep in all ways, but only a few?"

"Well, I wouldn't put it exactly like that," Julie said mildly.

"I can't think about it anymore," Morgan moaned, clamping her hands over her ears as if shutting out the din of her own thoughts. She sat up and looked at her friend searchingly. "Why do I have such bad luck with men? Do you think a troll put a curse on me at birth?"

"Is that what trolls do? I thought they hung out under bridges and made shoes. Or is that leprechauns?"

"Is this your attempt at cheering me up?" Morgan asked, half smiling.

"How am I doing?"

"Marginally."

"I think you're coping very well. I would be devastated."

"I am devastated. I've had several hours to recover from the impact of my conversation with him. You should have seen me when I left Beau's place. I was crying in the elevator, blowing my nose in the lobby, the whole bit. The last time I made that big a fool of myself was back in high school, when I broke up with Keith Canfield. Except with Keith I wound up crying during the basketball intramurals in the girls' gym, the one with the fluorescent lights that made everyone look dead. And this is ten times worse. I wasn't planning on marrying Keith, since we were both fifteen at the time."

Julie chuckled.

"The fates must have been in an antic mood when they brought me together with Beau Landry," Morgan said. She looked around the room. "I can't wait to get out of this place now. Philadelphia will look wonderful."

"I thought you loved New Orleans."

"I love Beau. He and the town are tied together in my mind."

"Still?"

"What?"

"You still love him?"

"Oh, Julie, do you think it goes away in a day? It wouldn't hurt so much if I didn't care so much."

"I know, I know." Julie pressed her lips together, then chose her words carefully. "You may not want to hear this, but I think you can salvage your relationship with Beau if you want to."

"I'm not sure I want to," Morgan said quietly.

"Why not?"

"Julie, he used me. If he plotted with Maria Aguilar and the others to recover the money and keep some for himself, he's a thief. And even assuming he's telling the truth about not taking any of the settlement, he has the ethics of Robin Hood. Can I make a life with somebody like that? If I go to one of those newspaper machines and the little glass door pops open to give me a paper without taking my quarter, I take the quarter and leave it inside the machine. If I go to the supermarket and discover that the clerk forgot to charge me for an onion, I bring it back. That's just the way I am. To say that Beau and I don't see eye to eye on a few things is putting it mildly."

"You seem to get along well in other areas," Julie said, smiling shyly.

"I can't spend my whole life in bed with him," Morgan said.

"If it were me, I'd try," Julie said, sighing.

Morgan ignored that, getting up and going to the mirror. "My God, I look terrible," she said in awe, staring at herself in the glass.

"I have to say you've looked better," Julie agreed.

Morgan shoved her disordered hair out of her eyes. "Well, I'd better get started on redoing my notes for the case," she said. "Think of me while you're dining with your date."

"At least I won't tell you to polish your nails or get your hair done."

Morgan shot her a look. "Thanks for that."

Julie went to the closet they shared. "I'd better take my shower," she said, selecting a dress.

"Sure, go ahead."

Julie looked over at Morgan, clutching the dress she was going to wear.

"Morgan, I really am sorry," she said.

Morgan nodded without expression.

Nobody was sorrier than she was.

Landry was sitting on his balcony, staring out over the river and drinking his dinner. He had downed two stiff scotches and was well into a third. The pain was receding into a sensation of numbing fog, but he was fairly sure that if he tried to stand up he would fall down. He planned to stay where he was for a while.

He had really blown it this time. He'd made mistakes before, but this was definitely the Super Bowl. Not only had he killed the Sunlite settlement for his friends, but he had lost Morgan in the process.

It was the worst day of his life. He'd felt pretty bad when his father died, but his father had been dying slowly for a long time. The break with Morgan was so swift, so sudden, that he was still reeling from the shock. Reeling right into the sauce bucket, he thought drunkenly, just like his old man. Oh well, what the hell. There was nothing to stay sober for anyway.

How could he have let this happen? Should he have abandoned his plans for the Sunlite case when he met Morgan and found that he liked her so much? Already, that first night at Antoine's, it was very hard to lie to her. The experience had put him in such a foul mood he'd almost ruined things with her before they'd started. But the number of people depending on him and the depth of their need had convinced him to go through with it anyway. And then he had fallen in love with the attorney from the insurance company he was trying to defraud.

There was an exquisite irony in there somewhere, but he was getting too plastered to nail it down precisely.

What to do now? he wondered. Jump over the railing and end it all? he thought whimsically. No good. He would bob to the surface like a cork. He swam instinctively, like a guppy. He would never be drunk enough to drown.

He could storm Morgan's hotel room. He's used that technique effectively before, but this time she would probably call the police. Not that he cared about being arrested, but it would be difficult to talk to her from a jail cell. He had to get her to listen, and he had never seen her so obdurate as she was that afternoon in his apartment. His task was to break through that wall, and he wasn't sure he could do it. He was confident, almost arrogant, by nature, but she was just as tough in a subtler, more selective way.

It was his misfortune to find that out too late.

He'd never thought his deception would be discovered, and he still didn't know how she'd managed it. She'd said something about a connection her boss had who'd told TA about his debts and started the two lawyers thinking about a motive for his testimony. And the really funny thing was that he hadn't lied for that reason at all, but it had led them to the correct conclusion anyway.

And all Morgan could see was that he'd lied.

Why did she have to be such an uptight moralist anyway? he thought savagely. It wasn't like he'd murdered somebody. The company pockets were deep enough, and guilty enough, too. He wouldn't have been taking money from an innocent source unable to afford it. But she was steeped in that "whole truth and nothing but the truth" mystique that all lawyers had drummed into them in school. Most of them forgot it pretty quickly, he thought sourly, but not Morgan. And it was costing him her love.

Well, he had to do something. He wasn't going to let her just walk out of his life, back to Philadelphia and into the arms of some Main Line type who wouldn't know the first thing about making her happy.

Establishing communication was the primary goal. He would send her flowers, that was it. Flowers with a note, asking her to see him. But first he had to get sober enough to use the phone.

He stood gingerly, and the summer night pinwheeled around him, stars cascading into the river. Whoops. He sat down again, hard. Coffee. He'd make some coffee, drink several cups if he could do so without scalding himself, and call an all-night florist. It was something, a positive step. One thing at a time.

In a minute he would try once more to stand.

Three days later Morgan was packing for the trip home. Julie was going through the drawers to see if they were leaving anything behind when a knock came at the door.

"If that's more flowers I'm sending them back where they came from," Julie said firmly. "This place already looks and smells like a funeral parlor."

Morgan stepped over a basket of begonias to get to the door. The room also contained three dozen roses, a gigantic spray of gladiolas, a wreath of carnations, and two vases of lilies.

When it came to making reparations, Landry did not have much imagination.

The bellboy was carrying a silver box bound with a silver-and-white ribbon.

"This came by special messenger," the boy announced. "Will you sign for it?"

Morgan signed the slip and took the box, reaching into her pocket for a tip.

The boy held up his hand. "You've given me enough already," he said. "This one's a freebie."

Morgan smiled. "Could you do me a favor?" she asked.

He shrugged. "What is it?"

"Could you arrange to have all these flowers sent to a hospital when we leave?" she asked. "It seems a shame to waste them."

"I'll check with my boss and let you know," he said. "It shouldn't be a problem; Gulf Memorial is right around the corner."

"Thank you very much," Morgan said.

The boy turned to go, and then said over his shoulder, "Somebody must really like you." He was grinning.

"Somebody is really sorry," Julie contributed from behind Morgan, holding aloft a scarf she had retrieved during her search.

"Goodbye," Morgan said to the kid, and shut the door.

"What is it?" Julie asked curiously, peering at the box as Morgan removed the ribbon. She lifted the cover and extracted several layers of tissue paper before coming to the object it contained. She took it out carefully as Julie whistled softly behind her.

"Gorgeous," Julie breathed. "Crystal, isn't it?"

"Lalique," Morgan said. She had once told him it was her favorite.

"That stuff costs a fortune," Julie commented.

It was a figurine of a nymph entwined with a satyr. At the base was inscribed the legend, "Love, and be loved, forever."

The heavy artillery, Morgan thought. Having hit her with all the floral arrangements he could buy, he was now moving up to Robert Browning. Talk about unfair tactics.

The enclosed card read, "At least you know the second part is true. Beau."

"What do you think it means?" Julie asked.

"I think it means he's giving up," Morgan said softly.

"No way," Julie said. "Not him. He's just exhausted the North American supply of cut flowers. This is a brief change of pace before the Brazilian orchids start to arrive."

Morgan put the crystal piece on the hotel dresser and resumed packing.

"You're not leaving that here," Julie said, aghast.

"I don't know."

"Well, I do. I'll take it if you don't want it. You're carrying this too far, Morgan."

"I didn't start it," Morgan said flatly, folding a sweater.

"If it were me, I'd talk to him."

"You keep saying that. It's not you."

"Come on, Morgan, look at all this stuff. Would he be trying this hard if he were as callous as you maintain?"

Morgan shook her head. "You don't understand. He thinks he can do anything he likes and then charm his way out of the consequences. All this is just part of the treatment. I'm not going to fall for it."

"Oh, no, not you. You're going to be strong and resist, and make both of you miserable in the process."

"It will be a change to resist him, don't you think? Look where trusting him got me. I was just lucky that Jerry didn't blame me for this Sunlite thing or I could be out of a job right now." She glanced at her watch. "What time is Bob coming to take us to the airport?"

"Four."

"Then we'd better hurry up. I don't want to miss that flight."

Julie stared at her for a second, then opened her suitcase.

It looked like they were both going home.

Ten

———

Julie knocked on the door of Morgan's office and then entered, saying, "Ready or not, here I come."

Morgan looked up, pen in hand. "What is it?" she said, still scribbling.

"Does Jerry know about these?" Julie asked, displaying two payment vouchers, tapping them into the palm of her hand.

"What are those?" Morgan asked, glancing down again, pretending ignorance.

"Don't give me that. They just came across my desk for your signature. You authorized two paralegals to investigate Sunlite's background."

"So?"

"One of them went outside the firm's files to the courthouse with instructions to detail Sunlite's litigation history for the past ten years, with particular emphasis on those cases in which it was sued as defendant. She's in the middle of her research now. I just finished talking to her."

"And?" Morgan said.

"You're not as convinced as you made me believe that Beau Landry's conduct was unjustified. You're looking to see if Sunlite was involved in anything like that oil rig accident before, aren't you?"

"I'm just trying to be thorough," Morgan said.

"Oh, bull. You're having second thoughts, and so you should. Sneaking out of town like that was a disgrace."

"I didn't sneak. I just left without telling him."

"You know he thought you were staying another day! Ignoring all those gifts he sent you wasn't very nice. And how many times has he called you since we got back here?"

"He's stopped calling," Morgan said quietly.

"Really? Disappointed?"

"Relieved."

"Hah. Tell it to somebody else." Julie leaned across Morgan's desk conspiratorially. "I wouldn't be surprised if he showed up in person one of these days," she observed.

Morgan shook her head. "He's gotten the message. He'll feel guilty about me for a while, but there are enough willing women around who won't give him the hard time I have. He'll forget me."

"You don't believe that," Julie said disgustedly.

"I have to," Morgan said, going back to her paperwork.

"You'll see him again at the trial."

"I'll worry about that when the time comes. You know how long pretrial motions can take."

"You miss him, don't you?" Julie asked knowingly.

"I'll get over it."

"I wonder."

Morgan looked up again, exasperated. "It might help if you weren't running in here every five minutes to talk about him. I would really appreciate it if you could just drop the subject and allow me to do the same."

"Very well, your majesty," Julie pronounced, in an imitation of Morgan's imperious tone. She curtsied with exaggerated deference and then swept from the room.

Morgan sighed heavily and threw her pen onto her desk blotter. Picking fights with Julie wasn't going to improve her spirits. The truth was that she had never been more lost and unhappy in her life, and she couldn't shake the notion that despair was right around the corner, about to overtake her.

She had done the right thing; she knew it. But then why did she feel so lousy? She felt, inexplicably, as if she had let Beau down, instead of the other way around. Every time she'd refused one of his calls, her funk increased. By this time her secretary probably thought Beau Landry was a bill collector.

It will get easier, she told herself grimly as she picked up her pen again.

It must.

Beau Landry was sitting at his desk, staring out the window of his office. He had a stack of phone messages to return, but instead he was wasting time, debating whether or not he should book a flight to Philadelphia.

It was clear that only a personal confrontation stood a chance of affecting Morgan's attitude, but somehow he couldn't make himself lift the receiver to call the airline.

He was afraid. He couldn't face a further, and final, rejection. Her refusal to speak to him long distance was one thing. But seeing her in person and hearing her tell him that it was really and finally over was another.

She'd been gone for two weeks now, and each day was an agony of self-recrimination. When he found that she had left early without telling him he knew that his task was formidable, but he still couldn't resign himself to the awful knowledge that he had lost her for good. There had to be something he could do. Otherwise, why go on?

The phone at his elbow buzzed.

He frowned, lifting the receiver. "What?" he barked.

"Pete Darriet is on line two," Yvonne Hastings said quickly. "There's a problem with sinking the tank at the Coleman site. They might have to blast into the rock bed."

What wonderful news, Landry thought, closing his eyes wearily. Blasting meant expense, danger, delays. It was shaping up to be another great morning.

"Put him through," Landry told the secretary, and punched a button on his phone.

He could call the airline later.

"Sit down, Joyce," Morgan said to the paralegal, indicating her conference chair.

The girl dropped into it, holding a file and a yellow ruled pad on her lap. She was detail-oriented, a thorough researcher. Morgan had assigned her to her current task for that reason. If anything were to be found regarding Sunlite's past, Joyce would find it.

At the moment her expression was not cheerful.

"What's the matter, Joyce?" Morgan asked.

Joyce swallowed. "Mr. Sinclair is planning to take the Sunlite case to court, isn't he, Miss Taylor?" she asked warily.

"Yes."

She tapped the file she was holding with a polished fingernail. "He's not going to like this."

"What?"

Joyce opened the manila folder. "I researched Sunlite's litigation history in the court files, like you asked."

"And?"

Joyce looked up at her. "Did you know that some of that history is missing from our files here at TA?"

Morgan didn't answer for a moment. Then, "What do you mean?"

"I mean that our internal files have been edited to exclude the reports of previous negligence cases like the one we're now defending. Miss Taylor, when Sunlite was with its previous insurer, Global Trust, it defended five accident-injury claims and two accidental deaths. Global told the company to clean up its act, and when it didn't, Global dropped Sunlite."

Morgan was silent, taking it in.

"The reports are all there in the court files, but there's nothing in ours. How could that have happened?"

"How indeed?" Morgan murmured.

"Mr. Sinclair doesn't know about this, does he?"

"I doubt it," Morgan said dryly.

"Well, you'd better tell him. If we go to trial, the plaintiffs' attorneys are going to bring this up in a big way. They'll make Sunlite look like a bunch of buccaneers."

"Are you sure about this, Joyce?"

Joyce nodded vigorously.

"When does the gap appear?"

"About six years ago," Joyce said.

When TA acquired Sunlite as a client.

"Joyce, give that file to me. I'll go over it and make an appointment to see Mr. Sinclair. Thank you very much, you've done a fine job."

Joyce departed, leaving the results of her research behind. Morgan buzzed her secretary and told her to hold her calls.

She had some reading to do.

"Clayton Boone," Jerry Sinclair said in disgust, tossing the paralegal's file on Morgan's desk. He was sitting in the chair Joyce had previously occupied, looking about as happy as Joyce had when she was there.

"What?" Morgan asked, wondering why Sinclair was bringing up the name of TA's deceased chairman in this context.

"You weren't here when we acquired Sunlite as a client, but I was. Boone was dying to get that company, the retainer was huge, the biggest we'd ever brought in up to that time. He knew he'd never get it past the board with this kind of shenanigans in its background, so he must have cleaned up its act, presented it as a lot shinier than it actually was. We signed them up, and here we are today, with this mess on our hands."

"And Clayton, who caused it all, has gone to his eternal reward," Morgan observed.

"I hope he's in hell, the old coot," Sinclair said savagely. "God, this case has turned out to be a nightmare. What in blue blazes are we going to do now?"

"Settle. We'll get killed in court when this comes out."

Sinclair moaned. "If I show up with *another* amended plea at this stage of the game the plaintiffs are going to know something's up and ask for the moon."

"Then you'd better give it to them. Anything's better than having a jury listen to a long, drawn-out account of every injury case Sunlite has ever been involved in as a defendant."

"The judge might not allow the testimony on the other cases; he might declare it irrelevant," Sinclair said hopefully, brightening.

Morgan shook her head. "You know that's a long shot in a case like this, where such flagrant abuse is present. Besides, even if it were disallowed, the other side would find a way to make sure the jury heard it." Morgan put her thumbs into the lapels of her jacket and deepened her voice, pretending to be plaintiff's attorney. "Sir, are you aware that the defendant Sunlite has been sued in seven actions similar to this one in the recent past and made settlements to the amount of twenty million dollars?"

"Your Honor, I object," Sinclair said dutifully, playing his role representing Sunlite. "Plaintiffs' Counsel's question is irrelevant. Sunlite's past history has no bearing on this individual case and could be considered prejudicial."

"Sustained," Morgan barked, now impersonating the judge. "Plaintiffs' Counsel's question is improper and will be stricken from the record. The jury is instructed to disregard it."

"And of course the members of the jury recall it word for word to their dying day and vote to return a staggering settlement for the plaintiffs," Sinclair said mournfully.

"You got it."

He stood abruptly. "Well, I'd better not delay. I'll tell you one thing. I'm going to need a vacation when this one is over." He grabbed the file from Morgan's desk. "I'll get back to you," he said, holding it aloft, and went through the door.

* * *

Julie came up behind Morgan at the coffee stand and said meekly, "Are we still on speaking terms?"

"Of course," Morgan replied. "I'm sorry about the way I acted earlier; I'm just a little edgy."

"A little," Julie agreed, watching as Morgan filled her cup from the pot on the warmer.

Morgan realized that Julie was waiting expectantly.

"What?" she said.

"Joyce told me," Julie said.

"Oh."

"What are you going to do?"

"We're going to settle."

"No, dummy, I meant about Beau."

Morgan shrugged. "What is there to do?"

"Don't you think he deserves to know that he was right about Sunlite?"

"That doesn't excuse what he did."

"Come on, Morgan, can you imagine the sort of things he must have seen on that Sunlite rig before the accident? We're talking about a company with one of the worst safety histories on record."

"I know that."

"If you'd been looking at that every day, working with it, you might have made the same decision he did. Especially when you knew that if you stuck to the literal truth Sunlite would get off scot-free."

Morgan didn't answer.

"I'll tell him if you don't."

"Don't push me, Julie."

"Are you going to call him?"

"No."

"Then what?"

"I'll write him a letter."

"Will you really?"

"Yes."

Julie studied her, then nodded.

"See that you do," she said, and walked off down the hall.

Morgan returned to her office and took a sheet of company stationery, deciding to make it a handwritten note rather than route it through her secretary. She deliberated a few moments before picking up her pen and writing.

Dear Beau,

I thought you would like to know that TA has decided to settle the Sunlite case out of court after all. New evidence has come to light suggesting that the company has been a habitual safety offender for a long time. We would not be able to defend the case, as Sunlite would be tried on its past record as well as the present facts.

You were right about the situation, but not about the tactics you used to handle it. I hope that this outcome makes you feel better about the accident and its aftermath.

Morgan read it quickly, satisfied. Crisp, impersonal, exactly what she wanted.

She scrawled her name at the bottom and slipped the single sheet into an envelope, sealing it and addressing it from memory. She took it to the outgoing mail basket and dropped it in with the company correspondence before she could change her mind.

That's that, she thought, and went back to her office.

* * *

Landry glanced at the pile of letters on his desk and groaned inwardly. Yvonne usually handled all the bills and junk mail and left the more important, and personal, mail for him. Today it didn't look like her efforts had diminished it much.

He sorted through it quickly, one eye on his desk clock. He was already running late and . . .

He froze with a cream vellum envelope in his hand. It bore the return address of TransAmerican Insurance Corporation, but it was addressed in pen. In familiar handwriting.

He tore the envelope open, his hand shaking. He scanned the few lines rapidly, then closed his eyes, his heart hammering loudly in his chest.

It wasn't much, but it was something. An olive branch, a ray of hope. He stood thinking for a moment and then buzzed his secretary, jabbing the button again when she didn't answer the summons immediately.

"Yes?" She sounded annoyed.

"Yvonne, I have to go out of town right away. Call around and cancel everything for a couple of days, will you?"

"You've got dinner with Councilman Thibodeau today!" Yvonne said, incensed. "He's been trying to get to see you for three weeks. What am I supposed to tell him?"

"Tell him I got called away on an emergency and reschedule it at his convenience."

There was silence.

"Yvonne, will you do that for me?"

He heard a profound sigh.

"All right," she said.

"And see if you can schedule a flight for me this afternoon. I want to leave as soon as possible."

"Where are you going?"

"Philadelphia."

On the other side of the wall, Yvonne raised her eyes heavenward. Oh, no. He was starting up with that lady lawyer again.

"Yvonne?" he said.

"I'll get right on it."

Landry hung up the phone and began to read Morgan's letter once more.

Julie was photocopying documents in Morgan's office when the phone rang. She shut off the copying machine and went to Morgan's desk, picking up the receiver.

"Yes?"

"There's a man here to see Miss Taylor," Morgan's secretary said. "He doesn't have an appointment, and he wants to wait. I told him that Miss Taylor was in court and wouldn't be back for several hours, maybe not for the rest of the day, but he insists on staying."

"Who is it?" Julie asked.

"Beauregarde Landry," the secretary replied. Then she added, sotto voce, "That's the one who was calling her all the time, remember? Miss Taylor would never take his calls."

"I'll see him," Julie said, smiling to herself. "Send him in."

"But are you sure that would be all right with Miss Taylor?" the secretary asked worriedly.

"It will be all right. I'll take responsibility. Send him in."

Seconds later the door opened and Beau Landry walked through it. He was wearing a short-sleeved, white cotton sweater, tan slacks, and loafers.

He was as devastating as Julie remembered.

"Hi, Julie," he said, and smiled.

"Hi, Beau."

"How've you been?"

"All right. And you?"

He shrugged. "I hope to be better soon. Is it true that Morgan isn't here?"

"She really is in court, Beau."

"I thought it was just another dodge."

"I think she'll see you now."

He eyed her intently. "You do?"

"Yes."

"I came because I had a letter from her."

"I've been expecting you to show up sooner or later."

"I had to come here. I don't know where she lives."

"Really?"

"The subject never came up, and then after we had that falling-out she wouldn't even talk to me."

"I remember." Julie shot him a sidelong glance. "By the way, I enjoyed the avalanche of flowers."

"More than Morgan did, I bet."

"She was hurt, Beau."

"I know it," he said softly, looking over Julie's head at nothing. He was silent a moment, thinking, and then added, "I am so sorry."

"I believe you."

He smiled ruefully. "The question is, does Morgan?"

"I know how you can find out."

He watched her alertly.

"I have an extra key to her apartment, which is only a few blocks from here. Why don't I give you the directions and you can let yourself in and wait for her? You'd certainly have more privacy than you would in this barracks."

"Would you do that?" he asked quietly, unable to credit this good fortune.

"Sure. She'll be in court the rest of the afternoon. She'll go home afterward, I think."

"She'll be furious with you if she doesn't want to see me."

"She wants to see you. She's just having a little trouble admitting it." Julie reached into her purse and took out a key ring, extracting one of the keys from the metal circle and holding it up in the air like a contest prize.

Beau eyed it greedily.

"It's yours," Julie said, and he took it.

"Thanks a lot," he said, bending to kiss her cheek.

"Don't mention it," Julie replied, flushing.

"How's your life going?" Landry asked, feeling obliged to make small talk. He really wanted to dash for the door with the key in his hand like a relay runner with a baton.

"My life is fine. Now will you get out of here? Take a left at the front door and go two blocks south to Delancey. Turn right there onto Crossbridge. It's the second brownstone on the left. Morgan has the first floor. Her name is on the box. It's close; you can walk it."

"I think Morgan has a very good friend. I know I do," Landry said huskily.

He's a charmer, all right, Julie thought. Morgan, look out.

"Get out of here," Julie said.

He left.

Julie got up and resumed her photocopying, humming to herself.

Landry found Morgan's building with no trouble; Julie's directions were exact. It was a small two-story brick row house tucked in with others like it, with a white lintel around the red front door and a tiny front porch. He unlocked the door, almost staggering with fatigue. He'd had trouble making plane connections and had spent a sleepless night in airports.

The apartment was like Morgan, spare and practical, but with sudden touches of romanticism. The front door opened into a living room with a kitchen behind it and a bedroom off to one side. The living room was cheerful and bright, with sheer priscilla curtains across the double window and chintz covers on the sofa and chairs. It was filled with books. A shelf of porcelain collectibles stood out from them, creamy, fragile. The kitchen was big enough to contain a round ice cream table with two wrought-iron chairs, and the bedroom had a well-worn maple set that she might have brought from her parents' home. There was a picture of them on the dresser, a middle-aged couple with a large black dog sitting at their feet.

Pitch was the dog's name. Morgan had told him all about Pitch. He slept under her mother's bed with only his nose sticking out and collapsed across the threshold of the front door when he wanted a walk. You had to step over him to get out.

Morgan, he thought, clenching his fists. She was so real in this place that he could almost touch her.

He had to get her back.

Landry sat on the sofa to wait. After a while he decided to stretch out, just to ease his aching muscles.

In minutes he was asleep.

Morgan realized that her door was not locked when she inserted her key into the chamber. She hesitated, wondering if she had forgotten to lock it that morning, and then proceeded inside cautiously, ready to flee.

She stopped short, almost dropping the grocery bag she was carrying, when she saw a man supine on her living-room sofa.

It was Beau. He was sleeping soundly, one hand draped across his middle, the other trailing to the floor.

How on earth? she thought wildly, and then it came to her. Julie. Miss Cupid's Quiver, possessor of a duplicate key to her apartment, had set her up.

Morgan put down the grocery bag and crept into the living room slowly, careful not to wake him. She knelt next to the sofa, studying his sleeping face.

The long lashes she remembered lay against his cheeks, curling upward at the tips like a child's. His lips were parted slightly, and his black hair fell over his forehead in a deep comma.

There was no way she could resist this man a second time.

She touched his face. "Beau."

His lashes lifted. He stared at her in dreamy confusion for a moment, and then he opened his arms.

She slid into them, snuggling against his chest.

"Am I forgiven?" he murmured.

"I have to forgive you," she answered. "I can't live without you."

"Good," he said hoarsely, and kissed her.

Morgan responded, but when he started unzipping her skirt she stayed his hand.

"Wait a minute," she said.

"I've waited too long already." But he stopped, twining his fingers with hers.

"What are you doing here?"

"I came to see you."

"I gathered that much."

He reached up to touch the tip of her nose. "When I got your letter I thought you might be feeling a little less angry with me, so I figured I'd try again. I went to your office."

"Where you ran into Julie."

"How'd you guess?" he said, grinning.

"Well, unless you've added lock-picking to your other talents or have recently made the acquaintance of my mother, Julie gave you the key to get in here."

"Bingo."

"I'm going to kill her one of these days."

"No, you're not. You're going to have her as your maid of honor at our wedding."

"Our wedding?" Morgan said.

"We're getting married, aren't we?"

Morgan stood and walked away from him. "I don't know, Beau."

He sat up, following her with his eyes. "Why not? Is it still because of the Sunlite thing?"

She didn't answer.

"You love me, don't you?"

"Yes, I love you."

"Then what's the problem?"

Morgan turned to face him. "Our views are so different, Beau. I would never have done what you did, not for any principle in the world. For me, telling the truth *is* the principle. Don't you understand?"

"Come here," he said, patting the seat next to him.

She hesitated.

He patted again.

Morgan surrendered and sat down.

"You'll teach me, and I'll learn," he said quietly, looking into her eyes. "Isn't that the way it's supposed to work in a marriage?"

"I guess so."

"Morgan, I'm not a criminal. Even you don't think that."

"No," she conceded. "But you do have some creative ideas about how to make things come out your way."

"All right, but in the future I'll check with you before I do anything too bizarre, okay?"

"I'm not sure I should agree to that statement. How do we define 'bizarre'?"

"I'll never be able to win a word game with a lawyer," he said, sighing. "Can't you just accept it on faith that I will take your feelings into consideration?"

"I suppose I'll have to do that."

He took her hands in both of his and said softly, "Morgan, I've been very scared these past few weeks since you left New Orleans. I've been scared that I would end up like my father and live that futile, hopeless life that he lived because he couldn't have the woman he loved."

Morgan listened, touched.

"Do you think I'm going to forget? I'll never do anything like that again. I wouldn't risk losing your love. I've been out of my mind wondering if I could ever repair the damage that I did. Will you give me another chance?"

"Yes," she whispered.

"Will you marry me?"

"Yes."

He lifted her hand to his lips. "I'll buy you an engagement ring as soon as I pay off the florist's bill."

Morgan jerked her hand away, pretending to be miffed. "What a thing to say. I didn't ask for all those flowers."

"Julie said she liked them."

"Julie is a sucker for romance. I'm sure the poor bellboy who had to lug them up to our room wanted to murder you."

"Much good they did me. You still wouldn't talk to me."

"I'm talking to you now."

He pulled her head down onto his shoulder. "Are you really going to settle out of court on the Sunlite case?"

"Do we have to talk about that?" she said, wincing.

"Sorry. But I would still like to see Maria and the others get something out of it."

"They will."

"And I'd like to see me get you."

"You will."

"How about right now?" he asked, sliding his hand into the waistband of her skirt.

Morgan closed her eyes. "Now sounds good."

He undressed her and then himself, and made love to her on the sofa. They were entwined in dreamy lassitude afterward, savoring their closeness, when Morgan glanced toward the door and noticed a puddle forming beneath the grocery bag she had abandoned an hour earlier.

"Oh, no," she said, sitting up.

"Where's the fire?" Beau muttered, opening his eyes.

"The ice cream is melting."

"The ice cream?"

"I left it in the bag," Morgan explained, putting on his shirt and running for the hallway. The bag and its contents were a mess.

"Look at this," she mumbled, going to the kitchen and dumping the sticky items into the sink. "Double chocolate chip, too, my favorite."

"I'll get you some more," Beau said, coming up behind her and kissing the back of her neck. "Triple chocolate chip, quadruple, septuple."

"Septuple?" she said, giggling.

"Yeah, that's when each of the chips has six baby chiplets attached to it, like jimmies."

"You are an idiot," Morgan said, turning to face him and hooking her arms around his neck.

"Let's go into the bedroom," he said.

"Again?"

"What do you think?"

"I think we should go into the bedroom."

* * * * *

 Silhouette Desire

COMING NEXT MONTH

#451 DESTINY'S CHILD—Ann Major
Book Two of *Children of Destiny*. Ten years ago Jeb Jackson had become Megan MacKay's most hated enemy—but he was still the man she'd never stopped loving.

#452 A MATCH MADE IN HEAVEN—Katherine Granger
Film reviewers Colin Cassidy and Gina Longford were at odds from the moment they met. The sparks between them were dynamite on television and explosive off!

#453 HIDE AND SEEK—Lass Small
When Tate Lambert had uncharacteristically thrown herself at Bill Sawyer, he hadn't been interested. Two months later he had a change of heart, but apparently so had she....

#454 SMOOTH OPERATOR—Helen R. Myers
Camilla Ryland checked into Max Lansing's tropical island resort to get away from it all. But Max was a smooth operator, and he wasn't about to let the beautiful actress "get away" from him.

#455 THE PRINCESS AND THE PEA—Kathleen Korbel
Princess Cassandra led a fairy-tale existence before she met the handsome undercover agent Paul Phillips. He'd rescued her from danger, and now they were fleeing for their lives.

#456 GYPSY MOON—Joyce Thies
The third of three *Tales of the Rising Moon*. Veterinarian Robert Armstrong didn't intend to get involved with a wild gypsy woman. But then he met Serena Danvers and fell under her spell.

AVAILABLE NOW:

Silhouette Desire ®

CHILDREN OF DESTINY

A trilogy by Ann Major

Three power-packed tales of irresistible passion and undeniable fate created by Ann Major to wrap your heart in a legacy of love.

PASSION'S CHILD — September

Years ago, Nick Browning nearly destroyed Amy's life, but now that the child of his passion—the child of her heart—was in danger, Nick was the only one she could trust....

DESTINY'S CHILD — October

Cattle baron Jeb Jackson thought he owned everything and everyone on his ranch, but fiery Megan MacKay's destiny was to prove him wrong!

NIGHT CHILD — November

When little Julia Jackson was kidnapped, young Kirk MacKay blamed himself. Twenty years later, he found her...and discovered that love could shine through even the darkest of nights.

Don't miss PASSION'S CHILD, DESTINY'S CHILD and NIGHT CHILD, three thrilling Silhouette Desires designed to heat up chilly autumn nights!

SD-445